THE SECRET KEEPER

Elizabeth Carroll

The Secret Keeper

Published by Wheatmark®
610 East Delano Street, Suite 104
Tucson, Arizona 85705 U.S.A.
www.wheatmark.com

International Standard Book Number: 978-1-60494-245-3
Library of Congress Control Number: 2009922587

To my son Wesley, who proved that sometimes fantasy touches reality and dreams do come true.

" Dreams are the bright creatures of poem and legend, who sport on earth in the night season, and melt away in the first beam of the sun, which lights grim care and stern reality on their daily pilgrimage through the world."
—Charles Dickens, *Nicholas Nickleby*

The clouds drifted. Fluffy, wispy, fat, skinny. Bright white, each holding some beam of the sun.

The clouds floated. Solitary. Coupled. Spaced and jumbled.

The clouds glided. Over the green, across the blue, headed for nowhere and everywhere all at once.

The clouds rolled on. And carried with them an ancient secret.

Chapter 1

Tap-tap-tap.

The pen hitting the top of the computer desk kept the rhythm of impatience as fifteen-year-old Wil Johnson stared at his nearly completed essay. He glanced over his shoulder; the clock on his nightstand read 7:02 a.m. With a sigh, he glanced out the window. The morning sun peeked in at him, warm with the promise of spring. The tapping stopped as an idea hit him. He quickly wrote the sentences as his mom called upstairs, "Wil, Scott's here! Hurry, or you'll be late!"

"Coming!" He finished the essay and slipped the paper into his notebook. Then he slipped on his baseball cap and scooped up his books.

Downstairs, he found his best friend Scott Jenkins sitting on a bar stool, scarfing down a plate of French toast.

"Hey, bud," Scott greeted him; his green eyes twinkled mischievously. "It's good."

"Great," Wil moaned playfully. "Did you save me any, Mom?"

Nora Johnson smiled at her son. "Of course. Hat." She pointed to her own head. Wil quickly removed his cap, sheepishly running his hand through his brown hair. It fell boyishly across his forehead.

He took the plate she handed him and poured syrup on his toast. As he began eating, Scott turned to him.

"You do know the only reason I'm your friend is because of your mom's cooking. Otherwise, you have nothing to offer me."

"Jerk," Wil muttered so his mom wouldn't hear. His brown eyes danced merrily, though, in his boyish face that was neither round nor square.

"Mom, make Scott leave a tip," he suggested out loud.

"What? My charming company isn't enough?" Scott looked wounded.

"Don't you worry, Scott," Nora replied, running her fingers through her short, wavy hair. She tied a scarf around her neck. "I'll always have a place for you at my table."

"You are the best, Mrs. J." He winked flirtatiously at her. Wil made a gagging sound.

"Scott," Nora leaned against the counter and sipped at her tea, "I wish you'd call me Nora. You're practically family."

"Great, Mom," Wil complained. "Now we'll never get rid of him."

She smiled. "You two had better be off, or you'll miss the bus."

Wil swallowed his juice in one gulp and slid off the stool. "Bye, Mom. See you this afternoon."

"Later, Mrs. J!" Scott scooped up his catcher's mitt and trotted after Wil. Outside, the morning sun smiled down at them, her rays warming their skin and highlighting the flaxen in Scott's sandy blond hair as they walked to the bus stop.

"Hooray! Sunshine at last!" Scott cheered. "Now it feels like baseball season!"

"I thought you were game no matter the weather."

"I am. But it hurts when it's cold and you're throwing heaters. It's not like there's *much* extra padding here." Scott held up the mitt.

"Hey, you're the one calling the shots," Wil reminded him. "So don't be a wuss."

"Jerk," Scott grumbled as they reached the bus stop.

"So, did you do Ms. Frank's essay?" Wil asked, dropping his

bookbag at his feet so he could stretch out the kink in his shoulders.

Scott stared off in the distance and crinkled his nose. "Nope. Didn't have time."

Wil regarded his friend for a moment, then sighed. "It's your dad again, isn't it?"

Scott merely looked at him.

"You've got to tell somebody," Wil counseled. "Otherwise, you're gonna fail, and I'll have to be a sophomore without you."

Scott grinned, but the humor did not reach his eyes. "Like you could survive as a sophomore without me. Besides, I'll figure something out."

"Maybe you'll have time to rewrite it. I mean, English isn't til fourth period. It's not that hard to do."

"For you maybe. Let me guess. Yours is about which makes a better friend: a dwarf or an elf?"

Wil blushed slightly. "No, it isn't."

"What, then?"

"Never mind."

"You know I'm your best friend," Scott said diplomatically as the bus rounded the corner, "so this stuff doesn't bother me. But other people might think you're a bit mental if you keep on writing about dragons and leprechauns and wizards. We're in high school now. It's a whole different ballgame, or so I'm told."

"There's nothing wrong with writing about that stuff, especially from an analytical perspective," Wil defended himself.

"No, not if you're writing a book or keeping a diary. But we're talking homework here. People will *read* this. There's a big difference."

The bus pulled up beside them, and they climbed on. Wil didn't speak again until the bus was moving.

"I remember a time when you used to be just as interested in fantasy. You know, Merlin? Aslan? Gandalf?"

"Yeah, well, reality sets in really fast sometimes." Scott stared out the window.

"Come on, Scott. I'm just saying what if there is more to this world than what we get to see? What if there really is a place where time stands still and magic exists and mythical creatures run free?"

"You wrote about mythical beasts, didn't you?" Scott asked with a scrupulous look. "Which ones? The centaur? The Gorgon? The manticore? I got it. The sphinx. Nope, nope. The satyr."

Wil shook his head and ignored Scott's teasing. He watched as the school building came into view. Scott's opinion didn't concern him too greatly; neither did anyone else's. Wil had promised his dad on that bleak Saturday nearly two years ago that he would never let anyone dissuade him from being who he was or from believing in the unimaginable. "Dreams are what we get up for in the morning," his dad had wheezed, "and what we go to bed for at night. Never squash out a dream just because someone laughs at you or tells you it's impossible. Remember, son: 'Hold fast to dreams/ For if dreams die/ Life is a broken-winged bird/ That cannot fly.'"

Wil had those words hanging above his bed. He never went to bed at night without repeating them to himself. They comforted him somehow.

As the bus pulled to a stop and they gathered their things, Scott turned a concerned face towards his friend. "I do have one question for you though," he said as they made their way down the aisle. "You *don't* keep a diary, do you?"

Wil shook his head and shoved his green-eyed friend off the bus.

"Just checking," Scott replied as he shifted his bookbag. "Hey, there's Chris. Let's catch him."

They hurried after a thin, blond-haired boy who had just gotten out of a blue Volkswagen Beetle. He waved to them and waited for them to catch up.

"Hey, guys. How's it going?"

"It'd be better if I could get a little love from the cheerleaders

instead of you two bums," Scott answered, eyeing a pretty bru-
nette dressed in a cheerleading outfit. "Rah, rah, rah."

"You know," Wil spoke to Chris, "if they made cheerleaders a
subject here, he'd pass it blindfolded."

"Yeah, but where's the fun in that?" Scott asked as they walked
towards the building. "I like to *see* what I'm studying."

"Too bad you can't *see* your way to studying Mr. Lou's distance formula," Chris said with a shake of his head.

Wil noticed the haunted look cross Scott's face. However, his
bravado remained intact.

"I believe in the social scene. The only distance formula I'm
interested in is how close I am to Nina Selna."

"That, or a cheeseburger," Wil retorted, helping to keep the
mood light.

"Ha, ha."

"Speaking of distance formulas," Chris said as the bell for first
period rang.

"Yeah, yeah. I know," groused Scott. "Time for Lou's logis-
tics."

"See you guys later," Wil said as they headed away from him.
As they disappeared in the crowd, Wil turned and headed towards
his first class, science. He entered the classroom and sat down.
Beside him sat a plain girl. Her short brown curls were tucked
under a head band. Wide-framed glasses shielded her toffee colored eyes.

"Hey, Janet," Wil greeted her as he set his books down on the
lab table they shared.

"Hey, Wil. Hey, did you manage the homework problem
okay?" she asked. Her soft voice always comforted Wil. Science
was his worst subject, and Janet was a godsend. She managed
straight-A's in every class. Wil had known her since elementary
school.

"Yeah, I think so. I guess we'll find out when we mix the potion, huh?"

"It can't be any worse than Derek's. His potion exploded all over his hands. Lucky for him it wasn't harmful, although it did turn his hands a nice shade of Smurf blue." She chuckled.

"Did it come off?"

"Nope. Mr. Bent says it will, but it'll take a couple of days. Poor Derek went through, like, three bars of soap last night. Nothing worked."

Wil eyed his formula warily. "Maybe we should use yours."

"Don't be silly. I'm sure yours is just fine." She opened her text book, then glanced at his notes. "Buuuutt," she drawled hesitantly, "I'll be glad to look at it—"

"Yes, please." Wil shoved the notes under her nose as their teacher, Mr. Golden, walked in.

"Good morning, my little Einsteins. Everyone please clear off your desks, everything but your formulas."

Janet pushed Wil's formula back towards him. She grinned. "Nothing to worry about."

"Really?"

She nodded. Wil grinned at her and slid his goggles on over his eyes.

That afternoon, Wil walked into Ms. Frank's English class. Scott was already seated at his desk, staring unabashedly at the cheerleader named Stacey Jo. She busily ignored him, talking instead to a perky redhead with large brown eyes. Wil sat down beside Scott.

"Hey, buddy."

Scott made no reply. His focus never wavered. Wil stared at him, then glanced at Stacey Jo, then back to Scott. He shook his head and started pulling out his notebook.

"Here's what I've decided," Scott declared suddenly.

"Why do I feel an 'uh-oh' coming on?" Wil asked.

Scott ignored him. "Redheads are hot."

Wil glanced at the red-haired girl sitting behind Stacey Jo. "I think he means you, Laurie."

Laurie giggled. "You're sweet, Scott."

Scott beamed.

"Ewww!" Stacey Jo rolled her eyes.

"You're really pathetic, you know that?" Wil asked as he twirled his pencil in his fingers.

"Me? Pathetic? Maybe." Scott turned his attention from the two girls. "But at least I'm digging the realistic things. You have a thing for what? Unicorns? Frankly, *I'm* worried about *you.*"

Wil turned to make a reply, but Scott's attention was drawn away by the entrance of a new person.

"My man!" he called out jovially. "Looks like you're suffering a temporary case of the blues!"

Wil laughed as the newcomer sat in front of him.

"Very funny," the boy said as he splayed his heavily blue tinted hands in front of them. "This stuff is like permanent glue. I had to have scrubbed my hands for at least thirty minutes straight last night. Nothing worked."

"Well, Derek, look at this way," Scott replied. "At least no one can accuse you of not having school spirit."

Stacey Jo giggled.

"He's not very comforting, is he?" Derek asked Wil as a young woman in her thirties walked into the room.

"No, he's not."

"Good afternoon, class. If you will please take out your homework assignments, we'll begin," the young woman instructed.

Wil pulled his paragraph out of his notebook. Out of the corner of his eye, he noticed Scott doing the same thing. He glanced at his friend. Scott shrugged. "It is what it is," he informed Wil.

Wil shook his head. His attention was drawn towards the knock at the door. Wil was aware of the absolute stillness of the room when *she* walked in. He felt his mouth fall open in amazement. Never mind the fact that the new girl standing beside Ms.

Frank had the smoothest skin he'd ever seen on a teenager, pearly white, like thick cream; never mind the silkiness of her honey blond hair wrapped in a white cord; never mind the sheer innocence of her smile. None of that caught his attention at first. His disbelief stemmed from three things: first, the white robe she wore; second, the crystal topaz of her eyes; third and most importantly, she *glowed*. A radiant light seemed to permeate from the top of her head to the tips of her naked feet.

"Wow." Scott's whisper came very close to Wil's ear, and he realized his friend had leaned over for a better look.

Wil turned stunned eyes towards him. "Do you see her?" he asked in disbelief.

"What? Do you think I'm blind? Of course I see her. She is ... wow."

Wil shook his head, puzzled. He wanted to press the issue, but at that moment, he became aware that every boy in class was fixated on the new girl.

Wil glanced around. The girls waited politely for Ms. Frank to introduce the newest member of the female clan; the boys ogled.

All, except one. In the back corner of the room, his desk set apart from everyone else's, sat a boy with shaggy black hair and deep black eyes. His second-hand black jacket gave him a thuggish look, as did his dirty, chewed-up fingernails and furrowed brows. His expression was almost a glare. After a moment, the boy realized Wil was looking at him. He slouched down in his chair and scowled fiercely at Wil, a threatening look.

"Class, this is Cassia Cloud," Ms. Frank announced. "She'll be joining our little learning group. Cassia, you may take that empty seat there." She pointed at the empty desk next to Wil.

He froze as Cassia moved to sit beside him; it almost seemed as if she *floated* to the desk.

Wil rubbed his eyes and looked at her again. His eyes widened even further in disbelief, for now she sat in a long blue skirt and white blouse. Her hair was pulled up in a ponytail. The glow was gone.

He stared at her until she glanced his way. Averting his eyes, he stared straight ahead, inhaling and exhaling deeply once. Scott peered around him, still gawking.

"Stop staring, Doofus," Stacey Jo whispered as she leaned in. "It isn't polite." She thumped Scott on the shoulder before scooting back into her seat.

"Ow!"

"Scott," reprimanded Ms. Frank.

"But sh—" Scott held off on tattle-telling. He did give Stacey Jo an evil look, though.

"Why don't you come up here and read your essay to us?" Ms. Frank suggested.

Scott frowned more furiously, but he picked up his paper and marched to the front of the class, much to the amusement of Wil, Derek, and the girls.

"Ahem." Scott shook the paper in front of him as if it were an important document. "To see or not to see Italy. That is the question. I would really like to see Italy one day. Not only do they have the *best* pasta in the world, like spaghetti and macaroni and cheese, but they have these gorgeous girls that feed it to you on big spoons."

Several students laughed, including Wil and Derek. Laurie shook her head. Stacey Jo rolled her eyes and let out an exasperated, "Oh please!"

Scott continued undeterred. "Girls in Italy like to eat and they like to feed boys. Italian women are always saying how skinny everybody else is, so I wouldn't have any problem fitting in because I would eat whatever they wanted to feed me. And it would be cool to have a different girl to feed food to me each day. So I really, *really* want to see Italy. The end."

Scott sat back down; Wil noticed that behind the triumphant heroics lurked shame. He marveled that Scott could keep it so well hidden.

Ms. Frank looked amused. "Well, you did the assignment today. That's a start, but let me ask you. Was that really an essay?"

"I like to think of it as a work in progress," Scott replied with a grin.

"Mmm. Well, let's see if we can progress it into a three paragraph essay with a few more, um, scenic facts by tomorrow," Ms. Frank suggested sternly.

"Just for you, Ms. Frank." Scott winked flirtatiously, then looked at Wil. "She really likes me."

"Like the plague."

"But a good plague."

Ms. Frank called on Derek to read next.

"All right, Smurf Man!" Scott called out as Derek took his stance in front of the class. Ms. Frank gave him a look. "Sorry, Ms. Frank."

As Derek began reading his paragraph, Wil read through his essay once to make sure there weren't any mistakes. Suddenly, he became aware of a sweet scent, cinnamon and apples, tickling his nose. He looked up and his attention caught on Cassia sitting to his right. He stole a glance at her out of the corner of his eye, then turned to stare at her. She wasn't so much sitting in the desk as hovering above it. Her attention was focused on Derek; she listened to his report with great interest. Plus, the glow was back as was the white robe.

Wil felt faint with disbelief. He stared, unable to look away. Even when Cassia turned her crystal blue eyes on him, he couldn't pull his gaze away. Her calm, interested expression turned to one of puzzlement as they surveyed one another.

"Wil."

"What?" He blinked and looked at his teacher, his heart hammering hard. Was he about to be reprimanded? Had Ms. Frank seen the glowing girl?

"It's your turn," she said, motioning towards the front of the class.

He glanced back at Cassia. She sat in the desk, her white blouse and blue skirt illuminated by nothing more than the fluorescent lighting from overhead. The fragrance of cinnamon apples had disappeared. Her bewildered look followed him to the front of the class.

Wil forced his eyes on the paper in front of him. *Just start reading*, he told himself, and with a deep breath, he did.

"Belief in the impossible is part of the formula for a happy life." He swallowed once to moisten his suddenly dry throat. "Too often, kids lose their belief in childhood fantasies, like Santa Claus and the Easter Bunny. Kids grow up too fast, it seems. Sometimes it's because we're expected to, and sometimes it's because we have to. But my dad once told me that it's okay to keep believing in the unbelievable. It makes life more bearable, and sometimes it makes it more fun.

"Maybe that's why fantasy stories have become so popular. People like J.R.R. Tolkien and C.S. Lewis have been around forever, but there have only just been big movies made based on their stories, and the movies did really well. Then there's the Harry Potter collection which has also been turned into really successful movies. It could be because they are just really good stories, but it could also be because sometimes life is just too hard, and people want to be able to escape to a time when there were elves and witches and dragons, where good always triumphs over evil. Sometimes as adults, people want to go back to being kids; they want to believe in Santa Claus at Christmas time and they want to believe that they can fix anything with a wave of a wand.

"Keeping hold of fantasies keeps life from getting too dull. People want to be able to believe in magic and unicorns when life gets hard. Believing in places like Narnia or Hogwarts lets people keep hold of their childhood a little bit longer, no matter how old they are."

Wil finished and looked up. Cassia stared at him, her look at once considerate and perplexed.

Ms. Frank smiled. "Very nice, Wil. Thank you."

He nodded and scooted back to his seat. He made sure to keep his gaze on anything but Cassia.

"Andrew, would you go next, please?" Ms. Frank called out.

"Gee, I'd like to, Ms. Frank," a voice sneered from the back of the room, "but I just don't know that I could top the elves and unicorns essay. I might be just a little too … grown up."

A few kids laughed. Scott turned in his seat and glared at the boy with the shaggy black hair.

"Shut up," Stacey Jo ordered. "I liked it."

"'Course you did. You're a girl," the boy from the back of the room said. "Fantasies are for sissies."

Wil tried to ignore the taunts. He did slouch a little further in his seat, though. He could feel someone staring at him. Out of the corner of his eye, he noticed Cassia watching him, her head tilted to the side, puzzling.

"At least he has some imagination," Scott defended his friend as Wil covered his eyes with his hand and scooted even lower in his chair. "He doesn't have to copy stuff out of books."

Andrew started to bow up. Something up front, however, seemed to catch his attention. He settled back in amazement as Ms. Frank stilled the classroom.

"All right, guys. That's enough. Scott, turn around. Andrew, I appreciate all input from my students, but I would ask that you try to be a little more helpful in your criticisms. By the way, we're still waiting to hear from you."

Seeming to recover from whatever had stilled him a second ago, Andrew retorted, "Yeah, well, I ain't got mine."

"I see. In that case, I suggest you not knock other students for doing their work, at least not until you start producing some yourself. Good job today, everyone. Read 'The Necklace' tonight for homework and answer the six questions at the end of the story. We'll discuss it tomorrow. Everyone turn in your essays before leaving."

Just then, a bell rang.

"Wil? Wil." Scott snapped his fingers in front of his friend's face, drawing Wil's attention.

"Huh?"

"You planning on spending the night here?"

Wil glanced around the classroom. Cassia was gone. He followed Scott into the crowded hallway.

"Boy, that was the most bizarre thing I've ever seen," he commented as they made their way to their lockers.

"What was bizarre?" Scott demanded. "Andrew's always a jerk. It would be bizarre if he wasn't."

"Not Andrew. Cassia. The new girl."

"Oh, man! She's not bizarre. She's ... wow!"

"You've already said that," Wil replied. "Didn't you *see* her, though? She was ... *glowing.*"

Scott paused and considered. "I've never heard it described that way before." He shrugged. "I would have said pretty, no, good-looking, no—"

"That's not what I mean," Wil interrupted as they reached their lockers. "I mean she was literally glowing."

Scott shook his head, amused. "Man, I think that essay has gone to your head. People don't glow, Wil. Well, unless you count pregnant women. They're supposed to ... emit some kind of light or something, but she was definitely not pregnant."

"No." It was Wil's turn to shake his head. "Okay, forget that. What was she wearing?"

"Clothes." Scott popped the lock on his locker and threw all of his books inside except for his English book.

"What kind?"

"Girl clothes, Wil. I don't know. A skirt, sandals. I wasn't really paying attention to her clothes."

"Wrong. She was wearing a robe. Well, at least part of the time. And you had to see her hovering over her desk."

"What?"

"I swear she was."

"Wil, people don't hover. At least not off the ground."

"Well, what about the smell, like cinnamon apples?"

"All I could smell was the soap from gym class." Scott shrugged at him as Derek caught up with them.

"Oh, man, did you guys see the new girl? What was her

name?" he asked, his blue hands busily stuffing a book into his book bag as he walked.

"Cassia. Yeah, we saw her. 'Course, Wil thinks she *glowed*," Scott teased.

Derek slung his book bag over his shoulder. "Nah, I'd have said ... cute?"

"No way. What about ... beautiful?"

"No. Attractive?"

"No, she's more than that," Scott reasoned as the three boys passed Laurie and Stacey Jo at their lockers. "What's a synonym for pretty?"

"Um, beautiful, gorgeous, lovely," Laurie listed. Wil sighed.

"That's it!" Scott exclaimed. "She's *lovely*." Derek nodded in agreement.

"Who is?" asked Stacey Jo.

"The new girl, Cassia," Derek answered.

"Oh, she was all right. Hey, Wil, I hope you're not gonna let that creep Andrew get to you. I really did like your essay."

"Thanks, Stacey Jo." Wil blushed and ducked his head shyly.

"I don't think he's really a creep," Laurie said as they stepped out into the afternoon sun. "He's sort of a bad boy. I kinda like that."

"Great. I'm sure Uncle Mike will be happy to hear that," Derek muttered. Laurie swatted at him.

"Well, Laurie, if you'd like to see some bad boys in action, you can come to practice with us. I'll show you my bad boy swing to right field," Scott schmoozed, putting his arm around her.

She giggled. "You are cute, but I promised my mom I would watch my little sister this afternoon. See you guys later."

Stacey Jo made a face at Scott as she followed Laurie down the steps.

"Dude, she's my cousin," Derek complained as the boys made their way down to the field.

"Yeah, I know. I'm still not sure how genetics worked there."

"Ha-ha."

Scott turned towards Wil. "What's the matter, Wil? Still thinking about your glowing girl?"

"No," Wil retorted, although he very much was thinking about her.

"You know, it's okay to admit you like her. That's how it's supposed to work."

"That's not it." Wil looked at both of them. "You swear you didn't see anything... unusual about her?"

"I swear," Scott replied emphatically as Derek shook his head. "She's just a really lovely girl. *Really* lovely."

Wil grew quiet as he contemplated the last ninety minutes of his life. Derek disappeared into the shelter to change clothes. Scott hung back, working his catcher's mitt.

Wil sighed. "I sound like a freak, don't I?"

"A little bit of one," Scott agreed, then punched Wil playfully in the shoulder. "Come on. I'll call sinkers."

Wil chuckled and trotted after Scott to get dressed for practice.

SITTING AT HIS DESK THAT night, Wil stared at the poster beside his window. The picture was dark and mysterious, enchanting and magical: the moon hung half in shadow, half a white orb against the purple and navy blue background; a waterfall cascaded from the lip of the moon, splashing brilliant white into the blue ocean beneath; mountains sat in shadow in the background, surrounded by thin wisps of cloud. A smattering of stars trickled down from above the moon, brushing against the dark side and growing brighter as they arched down upon the horn of a magnificent white beast, which stood large and powerful at the front of the poster. Seated in front of the beast was a girl in a flowing robe. She smiled up at the unicorn, her hand outstretched to rub its nose. Her face was half-hidden by hair that flowed brilliant white and gold, kissed by the starlight (and perhaps the magic of the beast?), yet Wil imagined great beauty and radiance concealed behind her hair.

On the other side of his window hung a poster of a map of Tolkien's Middle-Earth.

Above his bed hung Langston Hughes's poem. On his night-stand sat two dragon figurines: one blue, seated, with a white orb in its claw; the other one red, curled up asleep. A picture of a young boy and his dad, baseball gloves on their hands, sat be-tween the two dragons.

Wil's attention drifted back to the unicorn poster. He imag-ined the purity of the place, the harmony that existed between the girl and the unicorn. What would it be like to live in such a place? Surely, there would be no pain, no loss. There would be no death.

No death.

His dad would still be alive.

Wil shrugged off the longing and flipped off his computer. A secret place in the universe...

And then there she was, floating in his mind, the girl from English class. Wil glanced around, startled by her sudden appear-ance in his thoughts. After a moment, he chuckled to himself. *Maybe Scott is right*, he thought. Maybe, just maybe, it was an in-fatuation. Maybe he really had imagined the glow and gown and floating. No human could have emitted that sort of radiance, and certainly no human could hover that high off the ground.

He shut his literature book and tucked his homework inside his notebook. Crawling into bed, he picked up the picture of his dad and him. In his mind, he silently recited the words of the poem hanging over his bed.

"'Night, Dad," he added out loud before setting the picture back in its place. Then he reached over and turned out the light.

Chapter 2

The next morning, Wil walked down the hall towards science class. He rubbed his eyes as he approached the classroom door. What a bizarre night he'd had; all night he had dreamed of unicorns. Not that there was anything unusual in that; he had dreamed about unicorns before—and leprechauns and dragons and pixies. But his dreams last night had been more vivid than ever. The gentle pounding of the hooves had sounded so real, and Wil would have sworn he could feel the water droplets splashed out of the creek by the running unicorns. In the end, though, he had awakened to his same old bedroom. As with most good dreams, he felt immense disappointment upon waking. There was little comfort to be derived from his CD player or his CDs; even the pictures of his family on vacation at the Grand Canyon did little to soothe the discontent.

And now he had to face the dreaded science. He went inside and sat down at his table. Janet had not yet arrived.

Wil took out his textbook and notes. He stared at the beaker and Bunsen burner. He hoped Janet would make it in time to check his formula. He glanced around the classroom. The shades were pulled up, and the morning sun glinted off the windows. Outside, Wil could just make out a few clouds in the otherwise blue sky. Curiously, it seemed as though one of those clouds was drifting towards the window.

He turned back towards his notes and twirled his pencil in his fingers impatiently. Suddenly he was aware of an odor, pleasant and fresh and sweet, drifting around him and filling the otherwise tepid air of the classroom.

Looking up, he felt his heart leap into his throat. Cassia hovered in the doorway, her white robe brilliant in the light emitting from her. Her crystal blue eyes met his stunned gaze; she grew puzzled at his expression.

Wil's intense scrutiny broke as Janet plopped down beside him, somewhat breathless, as the bell rang the start of class.

"My mom was running late," she apologized as she took out her notes and book, "and Mr. Cooper is giving out detentions. I just did make—what are you staring at?"

Wil blinked and looked at her, then cut his eyes back to Cassia. She stood beside Mr. Golden, her yellow skirt and pale blue blouse a splash of color against the whiteboard. Wil rubbed his eyes and inhaled deeply.

"Wil, are you all right?" Janet asked, worried.

He looked up and considered his friend. Janet had sensibilities; she could help him make sense of what he was sure was the beginning of a nervous breakdown.

"I saw something," he began, but Mr. Golden interrupted him.

"Good morning, little Einsteins. We have a new student. This is Cassia Cloud. She will be observing today as you concoct the formulas you created last night based on the reading. Your grade will be divided up as follows."

As he wrote on the board, Wil forced his attention from Cassia, who now watched him with great curiosity. He turned towards Janet.

"What would you think if I told you I thought I saw a girl actually floating in English class yesterday?"

She stared at him. "I would think you were mental."

"That's what Derek and Scott said." He slumped a little in his seat.

"Wil, people don't float, at least not in the literal sense." Janet busied herself with her homework assignment as Mr. Golden turned back towards the class.

"There you are, my little Edisons. Now, remember, this is a three-part grade. You must successfully show mastery in each area to receive an A. If there are no questions, you may begin."

"Besides," Janet continued as she began measuring out the liquid, "don't you think that somebody else would have seen a girl floating in class?"

"That's just it," Wil whispered back. "No one else did. That's why I don't know if I was imagining it or if she was really—"

"Oh, Wil, watch out. You're adding too much—"

As Wil's mixture began to heat up in the vial, a pungent odor wafted up. Janet pinched her nostrils shut.

"Ugh! Rotten eggs!"

Wil stared wide-eyed at his assignment gone horribly wrong.

"What has happened here?" Mr. Golden asked good-naturedly as several students groaned and "Ewww"-ed out loud. "Ah, Mr. Johnson, a pinch too much sulfur there, isn't it? Well, now, no matter. You still have a chance to salvage your grade."

"Too bad he can't salvage that smell," someone in the back muttered, and several students laughed.

"Yes, yes, Mr. Archuro, pungency has a way of waking up the sleepy souls of science, doesn't it?"

The student scowled and remained silent. Mr. Golden turned back towards Wil.

"Many a fine chemist has mixed up the elements in the early days of study, Mr. Johnson. However, you may still salvage your grade if you can locate the error in your formula and correct it ... on paper. I'm afraid there's not much we can do about the mixture itself—except give it a proper flushing down the sink drain."

Buoyed by Mr. Golden's encouragement but still suffering the stings of embarrassment, Wil gave his teacher a timid smile and stood to pour the foul concoction down the sink beside his work space.

"Well, look at it this way," Janet consoled, though she still crinkled her nose at the lingering effect, "it could've been worse. I mean, rotten milk is pretty awful. And rotten meat is even worse. I say you got off okay, even if we do have to suffer with this rotten-egg smell."

But Wil didn't smell the pungent sulfur combination. At that exact moment, the scent of cinnamon apples wafted around the room again. He didn't have to look up to see its source, but he did anyway.

Cassia stood in her radiant light, watching him, a slight smile on her face.

The beaker fell from his hand and clattered in the sink. Cassia looked startled. Mr. Golden glanced up from the formula he was checking. Wil glanced at the sink—thankfully the beaker hadn't broken—and offered a weak smile.

"Sorry, Mr. Golden. Just having one of those days."

He quickly recovered the beaker, rinsed it out, and set it on a paper towel to dry. With a glance at Cassia, he turned his attention towards Janet.

"She's *glowing*," he whispered.

"Who?" Janet whispered back, questions etched on her face.

"Cassia."

Janet stole a glance at the girl at the front of the classroom.

"What are you talking about?"

Wil jerked his head up. Cassia stood as an ordinary girl in an ordinary skirt and blouse. Her eyes never wavered from Wil, and her perplexity began to change into concern.

Wil looked back at Janet. "I swear she was. She was doing the same thing in English class yesterday."

"That's who you were talking about," Janet reasoned, her voice low. However, she eyed him as though he was contagious. Wil sought for a way to convince her.

"There was a smell of … apples and cinnamon. Just now. Didn't you smell it?"

"Boy, do I wish I had! But I can't smell anything but what's left of your potion. Are you sure you feel all right?"

"I'm not crazy," Wil grumbled. Then, catching a look from Mr. Golden, he picked up his formula and stared blankly at the page. There was a lengthy silence at his table.

"I know you're not crazy, Wil." Janet spoke softly. "If you say you saw something, then I believe you."

He turned a relieved face towards her. She held up her hand.

"I'm not saying I believe you saw *her* glowing, but I believe you saw something. We'll figure it out."

Realizing it was the best he was going to get, Wil smiled his gratitude at his friend. "Thanks, Janet."

She smiled back. "Fix your formula." She nodded at the clock, which showed only fifteen minutes left in class.

With one last glance at Cassia, who had moved to stand by the open window, Wil pushed all thoughts of the mysterious girl out of his mind and concentrated on his erred homework.

WHEN THE BELL RANG AT the end of class, Wil had barely zipped up his bookbag before Cassia had disappeared out the door. Had he not been so preoccupied by thoughts of his insanity, he might have been tempted to look out his science classroom window, where he might have noticed a thin wispy mist of a cloud floating away from the open window, headed for the football field. He might also have noticed a fat, full cumulus cloud almost sailing across the sky towards the bleachers.

Slipping in between the stands, the misty cloud touched the ground and shimmered into the form of a young, honey blonde girl. Her white robe fluttered in the gentle breeze. A second later, the fat cloud slipped in between the bleachers and transformed into the image of a handsome man. He had thick, wavy brown hair and crystal blue eyes. He was dressed in colorful robes of sapphire blue. He smiled at her.

"Greetings, Cassia. The Council is interested in your progress. What do you have to report?"

Cassia spread her hands in a welcoming gesture and smiled. "This particular period in the lives of humans is consumed with mainly what they call 'education.' They attend these facilities, called schools, where they are taught history and literature and even how to create experiments, similar to what our own Samson does."

"I see. And what is the purpose of this 'education'?"

"This is the stage in human life where the young begin preparing for their futures, for when they are adults. It is through this education that the young humans gain knowledge, insight, and skills which they will further develop as adults."

He nodded. "Anything else?"

She nodded in return. "Not all of the young appear to enjoy this particular phase of their life spans. Some do exhibit the emotion enthusiasm, just as Samson described. They appear eager and interested to learn as much as they can. However, there are some who exhibit a less-than-positive attitude towards this education. I believe Samson described it as a feeling of indifference."

He arched his eyebrows. "I see. So even their young can be afflicted with this apathy. Have you seen any signs that Meslo's influence is at work?"

Cassia frowned. "No. These young humans appear to be just as complex as the adults. There is nothing in their actions to suggest that Meslo is responsible." She paused. "Is there a concern for that possibility, Charlie?"

He shook his head. "No. The Great Battle illustrated that Meslo's power is no match for that of Olin's. Still, it has been prophesied, so we must keep a close watch for signs. Is there any other information you wish me to take back to the Council?"

She hesitated and studied the grass at her feet. "I think I have been seen."

Charlie started at her words. "What do you mean? Were there any toddlers around?"

"No. One of these humans, I believe, has seen me."

"I do not understand. Samson assured the Council that humans at this particular stage do not have the ability required to see us."

"Is it possible that Samson erred in his assumption? I mean, even he does not understand why the toddlers are able to see us and humans at other stages are not."

"Yes. It is possible. Though we have been studying humans since the Great Battle ended, there is still much we do not know. As you have said, they are rather complex." Charlie seemed to consider an idea for a moment. "I believe it is best that you return with me at once. We cannot risk further exposure."

Cassia regarded him carefully. "I disagree."

Again, his eyebrows arched. "You know I speak for the Council. This is their will. Would you deny them?"

"Of course not but, Charlie, this could prove to be a valuable opportunity." She stepped forward, her hands spread before her. "Think about it. Here is a human who is old enough to communicate, and even more importantly, he can see me. We may be able to use this opportunity to have some of our questions answered."

"I do not believe that is a wise decision. You know what we risk if we are exposed."

"I do not think we will be exposed. There is something . . . special about this particular human. I have felt a connection with him. I cannot explain what that means, only that I believe if we are ever to fully understand them as a species, we need to be able to communicate with them. Besides, we have never had this opportunity present itself before. It may never present itself again. Please, will you not ask the Council? I will, of course, abide by their decision, but I think this could prove worthwhile."

Charlie studied her for a moment, his blue eyes serious. "It is worth considering," he agreed at last. "I will advise the Council and report their decision back to you. In the meantime, try to avoid contact if possible until you hear from me."

She nodded and watched as Charlie touched his hand to his forehead, then to his abdomen in a small arc.

"Til we meet again, Cassia." Then he vanished.

Cassia peered out from between the bleachers. A great fat cumulus cloud floated upwards, moving west of her location. After a moment, she walked out from behind the bleachers, her body slowly transforming into that perfect, wispy mist of a cloud as she moved towards the great blue sky above the lone football field.

WIL SAT AT THE LUNCH table, sipping despondently on his chocolate milk. Across from him, happily munching on French fries and pizza, sat Scott.

"That's disgusting," complained Stacey Jo from her spot beside Wil. She watched as Scott shoveled in a folded-over slice of pizza.

"Bm a bowing boy," he mumbled.

"What?"

He forced the food down. "I'm a growing boy."

"You're gonna grow right out of that seat you keep eating like that," Stacey Jo chastised as Chris and Janet joined them. As Janet sat down beside Scott, he surveyed her tray, then frowned.

"What is that?"

"Carrots." Janet opened her milk and sprinkled some pepper on her food.

"*Carrots?* Who eats carrots?"

"Not everybody wants blocked arteries, little piggy," Stacey Jo informed him.

"Yeah, but carrots? And what's that green stuff?"

Janet stirred her food. "Collards."

Scott groaned. "Now *that's* disgusting."

"How are you feeling, Wil?" Janet asked quietly as Laurie and Derek sat down with them.

He shrugged. "I just wish I knew whether or not I was going crazy. I mean," he leaned in to her, "that smell of apples and cinnamon. *Lots* of cinnamon. It had to be real."

"It probably was. I just don't know why. Look," she continued when he opened his mouth, "Wil, what you're talking about just isn't possible, not in real life."

"I know what I saw." Will remained adamant.

"I just don't know how. I mean, wouldn't other people have seen her glowing? I looked right at her. I didn't see anything."

Wil wadded up a napkin and looked away from her. He spotted Andrew sitting across the cafeteria, alone. There was no tray in front of him. He was staring off into space, his face neutral. Wil felt an unpleasant stirring in his gut when he remembered Andrew needling him yesterday in English class. However, Scott drew his attention from his nemesis.

"What are you two whispering about?"

"Nothing," Janet replied as casually as she could.

Scott furrowed his brow in disbelief and glanced towards Andrew. "You're not worried about that punk, are you?"

Wil shook his head. "No." He couldn't remain quiet under the scrutiny of his friends. "I ... had a bad experiment in science class this morning."

"Ooooh," Laurie breathed. "I heard about that. Juan Archuro said it really stunk."

Derek scoffed. "Juan sleeps through everything. If it woke him up, it *must* have been pretty bad."

"Don't worry about it," Scott waved concern aside. "Science is overrated anyway."

"So says the student with the 'D' average," Stacey Jo retorted.

"Hey! At least I'm passing."

"I thought you always checked his formulas," Chris said to Janet before taking a bite of his cookie.

"I was running late this morning," she replied. "Besides, it wasn't really his formula that was the problem."

Wil slouched in his seat. "I got distracted, okay?"

"Nina Selna!" Scott declared triumphantly, nodding his head in confidence and pointing a finger at his best friend.

"Ah, no," Wil replied as Stacey Jo sighed.

"Nina is so far out of your league, Scott, you couldn't touch her with a hundred foot pole."

"Not true. She flipped her hair at me this morning in math."

"Out of disgust, nothing else."

"Wil just … saw something. That's all," Janet explained over the bickering.

"What did you see?" Laurie asked as she arranged her trash neatly on her tray.

Wil toyed with the edge of his tray. "I saw … the girl."

"What girl?" Derek pressed.

When Wil didn't answer, Scott made a guess. "You don't mean Cassia? Of course! I should have known!"

"It's not like that."

"Then what is it like?" Scott asked, then immediately after, slapped himself in the forehead. "Oh, no. Not *that* again."

"Not what again?" asked Chris. "And who's Cassia?"

"She's a new girl," Derek explained, "a very lovely new girl."

"Okay, and?" Chris shrugged, still lost.

"And my buddy here thinks she glows, like magically glows," Scott explained, not bothering to keep the slight sarcasm out of his voice.

"What?" Chris laughed. "What is that about?"

"It's about an overactive imagination," answered Scott.

"Actually," Janet replied matter-of-factly, "it is possible, Wil, that what you saw was an angel."

Chris gaped at her. "An *angel*? In English class?"

"It's not unheard of. There have been many reports of people seeing angels, although," Janet pushed her glasses up her nose, "there are generally instances of great tragedy or stress that provoke such a sight."

"Maybe not," Laurie added. "I mean, my mom told me that my great-granddaddy saw an angel one time walking home from the bar."

"Well, that's self-explanatory, isn't it?" Derek scoffed.

"No. It's not like that," Laurie continued. "He was passing the cemetery and there was this great light, like a ball, you know? It was over a grave. I don't know if he thought anything of it or not, but my mom said that later that night, his daughter Jenny died. She'd had some respiratory problem all her life."

"Whoa. That's kinda creepy," Stacey Jo said softly.

"Okay, so what if it was an angel Wil saw? What does that mean?" Derek asked.

Janet shrugged. "That part I haven't figured out yet."

"I don't know," Scott frowned. "I still think you've been reading one too many stories, man. Glowing girls, angels, floaters, whatever you want to call 'em, it just seems … weird."

"All I know is what I saw, okay? And she smelled like cinnamon apples." Wil looked at the faces of disbelief around him. "Just forget it, okay?" He stood and picked up his tray. "I'll see you guys later."

"Nice going," Stacey Jo chastised Scott as Wil walked away. He put his tray up and turned towards the exit. Perched on the window sill overlooking the cafeteria sat Cassia. She stared right at him, waiting.

Wil glanced around; no one else seemed to have noticed. *Of course,* he thought. *I'm the only one going crazy.* He closed his eyes and shook the vision off. He would not give in this time. It caused him nothing but trouble. He opened his eyes just as someone bumped into him.

"Watch it, punk!" Andrew sneered at him.

Wil sighed. Over Andrew's shoulder, he noticed the girl had vanished. How convenient, and now, once again, he was in trouble.

"Hey, little fairy. Got any more unicorn stories for us?" Andrew teased.

"Look, Andrew, I don't have a problem with you, and I don't want to start any trouble with you."

"Well, ain't that too bad, 'cause I have a problem with you, and trouble? It's gonna be sitting on your back doorstep."

At that moment, one of the teachers monitoring the cafeteria strolled past the two boys. Andrew smiled smugly and gave Wil a not-so-friendly punch on the shoulder.

"See you later, little freak."

As he walked away, Wil sighed and ran a hand through his hair nervously. Then he left the cafeteria as the bell ending lunch sounded.

WIL SLOUCHED INTO ENGLISH CLASS that afternoon in a foul mood. His friends' flippant discussion over what he had seen had done little to relieve his worries. He knew it sounded strange, and he knew it made him look strange; however, he had been hoping that his pals would show more concern at the mystery. Instead, it had been nothing more than a springboard for speculation. And then there was Andrew who, no matter the occasion, always managed to make him feel like a freak.

He could feel the eyes of the others on him as he sat down and pulled out his notebook and pen. He did his best to ignore them; the last thing he wanted was to continue the discussion.

"Hey, Wil. Are you okay?" sympathetic Laurie asked.

"Yep."

"We didn't mean to make you feel bad," Stacey Jo added.

Wil scowled. "I feel fine."

"What did that punk Andrew want?" Scott asked.

"Yeah, we saw him in the cafeteria," Derek added.

"He didn't want anything."

He felt himself suddenly tense up when Cassia sailed into the room, her white robe fluttering around her naked ankles. The scent of cinnamon and apples swirled around the room, moving almost in rhythm to her movements. She hovered above her desk and looked at him, her expression calm.

Wil could feel the eyes of his friends on him. He saw Derek shoot a glance at Cassia, then look at Laurie and shrug his shoulders. Scott looked from Cassia to Wil and back to Cassia. He gestured hopelessly at Wil, who shook his head. Out of the corner of his eye, he saw her seated in the desk, her yellow skirt covering her sandaled feet.

The bell rang, signaling the start of class and bringing with it a moment of relief for Wil. He eagerly embraced the vocabulary lesson being given by Ms. Frank. As he worked, he noticed that Andrew had not yet made it to class; some of the tension in his shoulders eased. However, he chose not to join his friends in the group assignment Ms. Frank handed out, choosing instead to work alone. Scott tried several times to persuade him but eventually gave up when Wil ignored his efforts.

He kept his gaze on his assignment, sure that if he looked up, he would see Cassia's pen moving on its own, as if by an invisible hand, while she still hovered above the desk. This way, he could pretend he wasn't seeing it out of the corner of his eye.

As the minutes ticked by and the end of the day drew closer, a faint fragrance of warm cinnamon tickled Wil's nose. Without meaning to, he stole a glance at his friends. They talked amongst themselves, oblivious to the pleasant aroma. Wil returned his gaze to his work. He wrote his name on his paper, willing himself not to look up.

"Two minutes!" Ms. Franks called. "Make sure everyone in your group has put his or her name on the assignment. Pass the assignments to the front, please, and clean up your areas."

Wil handed his paper to Derek but kept his gaze down. Ms. Frank shuffled around, collecting the various assignments.

Casting a cautious glance to his left, Wil saw only the busyness of his classmates readying themselves for the three o'clock bell. Knowing it was inevitable, he slowly glanced to the right. Cassia watched him patiently.

Wil stared at her, this time determined to prove himself sane. After a moment, she smiled at him, and Wil felt suddenly lightheaded by the sheer innocence and warmth radiating from her. She glanced at the window and then back at him; her unspoken message wasn't lost on him, though the idea of speaking to her filled him with trepidation.

When the bell sounded, she seemed to melt almost into thin air. Wil stared in horror at the vacant seat for about two seconds. Then he snatched his bookbag and bolted from the room. He heard his friends calling after him but did not stop. Pushing his way through the throng of students crowding the hallway, Wil reached the side door exit and burst outside. Without a pause, he sprinted around the side of the building and ran the length of the wall, rounding the corner to face the back courtyard just underneath Ms. Frank's classroom. Pausing to catch his breath, he glanced around.

"Come on, come on," he muttered to himself. "Where'd you go?"

"Greetings, Wil Johnson."

He spun around. There she stood, in the flesh. She wore the same pure white gown and radiated the same lovely brilliance as the first time he had seen her. Her honey colored hair was pulled back in a spiral ponytail, its shape held by a white cord. Her blue eyes held him spellbound.

"Whoa. You are real," Wil said to himself, "aren't you?" He met her blue eyes again and found himself hoping she would say "yes."

She did. "Yes, I am real."

"So I'm not crazy."

She seemed puzzled by his question. "I do not have anything upon which to base such an idea. *Are* you crazy?"

Wil smiled nervously. "I don't think so. But I've got to know, what are you? Why is it that I'm the only one who can see you this way?"

She considered him for a moment, but all she said when she spoke was, "Fair questions, both of them. However, at this time, I cannot answer you."

"Come on," Wil pleaded. "You've gotta tell me something. My friends think I'm one step closer to a mental institution."

"Your words puzzle me, Wil Johnson. However, I cannot. I am bound by the will of the Council."

Now it was Wil's turn to be confused. "I don't—"

She glanced up at the sky. A great fat cloud drifted across the sky towards them.

"I must go now."

"No, wait!" Wil's frantic cry startled her. He took a deep breath. Either he truly was nuts, or else he'd made a discovery of unspeakable value. "One question. Answer me one question."

"All right."

Wil stared at her, his mind blank. She waited patiently; the fat cloud loomed closer.

"Um, well, uh, are you an angel?"

She smiled at him, and he felt warmed by her glow. "No, I am not. I must go now. It is time."

"Wait! One more question. This is... what you really look like, right? The glow? I'm not making that up in my mind?"

"No, you are not making that up in your mind, but no, this is not what I really look like. Farewell, Wil Johnson. Until we meet again." She touched her forehead and made an arc towards her abdomen. Then she transformed into a thin, wispy mist and drifted upwards and away from him.

Wil stared after her, his eyes bulging as they followed her up into the blue sky where it seemed she disappeared from sight. After a moment, he sat against the building, the bizarreness of the last few minutes washing over him. The last of the cinnamon fragrance faded, and the clouds seemed to drift away from the building, moving west, and still Wil sat.

She's real. She's really real, he told himself over and over. *And she said that she would meet you again. What does this mean? If I'm not crazy, then what am I? How is any of this possible?*

An invisible tickle brushed against him, much like a spider web. He brushed his arms and stood up.

Everything's going to be all right, he told himself. *Everything will somehow make sense.*

He shifted his bookbag. With one last glance at the blue sky, he left the courtyard and headed for baseball practice.

CASSIA STOOD IN A GREAT white room. All around her swirled the vapors of clouds; four great columns marked the edges of the vast room. In the center of the room, their chairs in an arc pattern, sat a Council of eight, all of them extraordinarily handsome with brilliant blue eyes. From her left sat Samson, intelligent, serious, with small round spectacles; Rebecca, whose pale blond hair shone in the bright light like gold topaz; Clover, matronly with skin the color of pearls; directly in front of where she stood sat Charlie and Jereni, whose red curls stood out in stark contrast to the whiteness of the room; Devlin, tall and thin with caramel-colored skin; Ballari, a small, slender woman with hair the shade of cinnamon, and finally, Rayle, whose thick, square face was covered with a red beard to match the hair on his head. To the far right of where Cassia stood lingered a large corpulent orb, dull next to the splendid alabaster of the room.

"So you freely admit to showing yourself to the human?" Clover questioned Cassia.

"Yes, but only after it became apparent that he had already seen me on several other occasions." Cassia stood quite confident before the eight.

"You do understand the consequences of our exposure to their world, do you not?" Ballari asked. She looked, in her smallness, almost obsolete in the vastness of the room.

"Of course, but I do not believe that such a risk exists."

"And from where do you draw this conclusion?" Ballari persisted.

"I have felt a connection with this human," Cassia answered. "He is open to such possibilities. I sense in him a desire—no, a *need* to believe in the unbelievable. I believe, if given a chance, he would be able to see the unicorns, dancing across the moon."

"Is that a possibility, Samson?" Clover asked the man sitting nearest Cassia.

Samson considered the question for a moment. "I must admit, I am puzzled by this latest development." He stood and addressed Cassia. "We have been studying these humans for many moons, what they call *centuries* in terms of their time. In all our studies, we have never risked exposure to the elder humans. The toddlers have ever only demonstrated the ability to see us, and as they have not learned the art of communication, they are easily persuaded that what they see actually does not really exist."

"And yet," Charlie spoke up, "here may be a chance to take our observations to the next level. We have the possibility of communicating with an actual human. Who knows what may be gained from such an interaction?"

"Indeed, there are great advantages to this opportunity," Samson agreed.

"And there are great risks as well," the lovely blond woman seated beside Clover pointed out.

"Rebecca is right," Clover agreed. "We must not act hastily, or we risk upsetting the Balance."

"I do not believe the Balance is threatened," Cassia said thoughtfully. "Wil Johnson appears to be the only human at this particular stage who has seen me. His friends have shown no such recognition."

The Council members looked at each other, silently considering.

"Should the Council consider allowing this observation to proceed," Devlin spoke after a moment, "how shall we garner a trust in this Wil Johnson? He is human, after all. He will talk."

Cassia stood at a loss for what to say. She glanced at Charlie, beseechingly. After a moment, Charlie turned towards the red-haired man seated at the other end of the horseshoe table.

"Rayle, you dusted him with the Feather of Forgetfulness, did you not?"

"I did. His memory should be cured of his encounter with Cassia," Rayle responded in a deep, gravelly voice.

Charlie took a deep breath. "Then I propose a thought for Devlin's question." He glanced at each of the Council members. "If this Wil Johnson truly believes, the Feather of Forgetfulness will have little effect on him. Should he recognize Cassia during her next observation, then perhaps we should consider trusting in his potential as a Secret Keeper."

Samson stroked his chin thoughtfully. "It would do well for us to re-establish that practice. We have not employed humans as Secret Keepers since The Great Battle ended."

"For very obvious reasons," Rebecca replied. "You will not forget, Samson, the betrayal of those Secret Keepers to Meslo. It very nearly shifted the Balance out of our hands."

"True, but not all Secret Keepers were in the employ of Meslo," Samson argued. "Some fought gallantly against his seductive powers."

"And perhaps we erred in our judgment," Ballari added. "Perhaps we should not have been so trusting in so many."

"True," Rebecca agreed. "We have lost quite a bit of information with the loss of our Secret Keepers. Perhaps it is time to re-establish that practice, but to make sure our identities are known to only a very few."

"Agreed," Jereni spoke for the first time. "Should this Wil Johnson retain his memory of Cassia, then he should be made a Secret Keeper."

"So says Jereni," Samson stated. "What say the others?" He looked at the rest of the Council.

Clover clasped her long fingers on the table in front of her. "I concur with reinstating the practice. But I would be remiss if I did not question the suggestion to use a human at this early of a developmental stage. As Rebecca has pointed out, the young humans do tend to be unable to suppress their knowledge from others."

"True," Devlin agreed. "And yet, Clover, we cannot deny what we know to be true about the adult humans. It was their ability to be controlled by lust and greed that allowed Meslo to seduce them many moons ago. Perhaps we will fare better by trusting the younger of the species."

"I agree with Devlin," Charlie spoke up. "Besides, it is only after their world convinces them that belief in the unbelievable is unacceptable that the younger humans give up those notions. Once innocence is lost, it is gone."

"And it would appear," added Rayle, "that this human, Wil Johnson, still holds a great deal of innocence. I believe we should trust that above all else."

"Are we in agreement, then, to allow the human Wil Johnson to serve as Secret Keeper provided he is able to counter-effect the Feather of Forgetfulness?" asked Clover.

The Council members each held up a hand, signaling a vote for the affirmative.

"So be it, then," Rebecca stated and looked towards Cassia. "Assuming this Wil Johnson has the ability to deny the power of Forgetfulness, you, Cassia, will become his guardian for as long as he serves in the role of Secret Keeper."

"I understand." Cassia replied, the small smile of success brushing her lips.

"Then the Council will reconvene at such time as the course of this plan is determined," Samson declared. Cassia nodded solemnly towards the eight before leaving the great whiteness of the hall.

Chapter 3

Wil sat at the kitchen bar, his math homework spread out in front of him. His mom, on the other side of the bar, cleaned the dinner dishes. She shook her head and chuckled.

"So what you're telling me," she grinned as she wiped dry a plate, "is that I shouldn't expect you to major in science in college."

Wil shook his head and wrote down an answer. "Definitely not." He looked up at her. "I'll leave the experiments to somebody else... unless they're going for that rotten egg smell. Then I might be able to help them."

Mrs. Johnson chuckled. "Any other adventures at school today?"

Wil returned to his math. "Nope. Same old stuff." Something tugged at the back of his mind, a faint, almost ridiculous memory that he couldn't latch on to.

He erased his formula and started over.

"You want some of these cinnamon apples for lunch tomorrow?" his mom asked.

Wil started and wrote down the wrong step. Taking a deep breath to quell the sudden fluttering in his stomach, he erased again.

"Sure."

"Need some help?"

He looked up at her. She was watching him erase. "Oh, no.

Just..." He pointed at his head. He corrected the formula and wrote down his answer.

Mrs. Johnson put the dried dishes up in the cupboard. "Teresa retired today, and I applied for her position."

Wil looked up. "Yeah?"

She shrugged. "I thought, 'what the heck?' I mean, I did pay for those night classes last year. Might as well put that knowledge to use. Besides, it's a better paying job, better benefits... and it's with the school system. If I get it, then you and I will have the same schedule, and maybe have some time to hang out... take a trip or go to the museum, you know, like we did when your dad was alive."

Wil wrote his name at the top of his paper, and then, because she was looking at him, he smiled. "That would be cool, Mom."

She returned his smile. "You know, you have the exact same dimple as your dad, right here." She pointed to her own chin and grew wistful. "Honey, I know this hasn't been easy for you—"

"I'm fine, Mom, really. I think we're doing okay."

"Yeah, we are." She looked as if she wanted to say something else. Wil waited, patiently; he knew how much his mom hurt, how much they both hurt. She had been great, though, not over-burdening him with her own grief but sharing it with him (in as much as he had let her).

She opened her mouth just as someone rang the doorbell. Relief and disappointment mingled on her face for a second as the doorbell rang again.

"It's okay. It's nothing that can't wait."

"Okay. I'll get that." Wil closed his math book and trotted to the front door. On the front stoop stood Scott, his backpack in one hand and a couple of video games in the other.

"Hey, buddy," he said as crossed the threshold. "Mind if I crash here tonight? Dad's hitting the bottle pretty hard, so I just wanted to get out of his way."

"Yeah, sure." Wil studied his friend. He seemed a little more subdued than usual. Although Scott had gotten very good at hiding the tough times behind wisecracks and jokes, Wil knew all too well the façade had cracks in it, and tonight, the cracks were showing.

"You okay?" Wil asked as they started down the hall.

"Yep. I brought game three for us, you know, to play. I finally made it to level seven."

Wil nodded and stopped in the kitchen long enough to get his books. He glanced meaningfully at his mom.

"Scott's gonna spend the night. Is that okay?"

Mrs. Johnson nodded. "Of course it is. Have you had dinner, Scott?"

He nodded.

"Okay. Well, there're snacks in here if you guys get hungry. Not too late, okay, fellas? School tomorrow."

"Okay, mom." Wil gathered his books. "Night."

He led the way upstairs. They stopped off long enough for Scott to throw his bookbag into the spare bedroom and then went to Wil's room. Wil uploaded the video game into his system, trying not to be too conscious of Scott's silence.

After a few minutes of play, during which Wil's character achieved level three while Scott's character repeatedly fell into the pit or was felled by a group of orcs in the woods, Scott set down his console and wandered over to the picture of Wil and his family at the Grand Canyon.

"I remember when this happened, this trip," he said after a moment. "It was the summer before we started middle school."

"Yeah." Wil concentrated on side-stepping the booby-trap his character had discovered.

"Your dad was a good guy." Scott studied the picture of Mr. and Mrs. Johnson. Almost to himself, he added, "It seems like all the good ones leave while the bad ones..."

Wil's character gave a yell as he was hit by a deadly curse. He glanced at the unicorn poster, a familiar longing creeping up on him. He reset the game.

Scott shook himself and turned away from the pictures. As he sat back on the bed, he glanced around the room.

"Dude, we have got to get you some bathing beauties in here."

Wil glanced at him. The old Scott seemed to be returning, and he shook his head, relieved.

"No room."

"Puh-lease. Replace Harry Potter. Better yet, put one on the ceiling. I've got one—Sheila. Bee-u-ti-ful."

"No way. That's creepy. Somebody staring down at me while I sleep."

"You want to know what's creepy? The banshee on level seven."

"A banshee? No way."

"Totally. Let me show you."

Outside the window, a full moon rose in the sky around which draped a thin, silvery wisp of cloud.

THAT NIGHT, WIL DREAMED OF banshees and angels, of liquor bottles and goblets of fire, of baseballs and broken science beakers. The images splashed across his subconscious, each reflection overlapping the other in brief succession so that fear never outweighed delectation, and bliss never surmounted the disquietude.

Wil tossed restlessly in bed. Through the dream haze of light and dark, good and evil, came a great white beast, starlight sprinkling from its horn. It stopped and stared at Wil, who was caught in his own dream. The creature's gaze was calm and innocent, and Dream Wil fought the urge to reach out a hand towards it.

From the shadows stepped a girl encased in a radiant white light. Her honey colored ponytail was held in place by a white cord. Her blue eyes glistened crystal clear as she stroked the nose of the beast. From within his dreams, Wil detected a hint of cinnamon and apples.

After a moment, she spoke, her voice lilting as a harp: "Do you know me, Wil Johnson? Can you still see?"

Dream Wil stared at her, uncomprehending. She waited patiently, her hand outstretched towards him.

A shriek sounded to his left, shrill and spooky. Dream Wil looked in the direction of the sound; his heart hammered at the wild-eyed, wild-haired female that came from the shadows. Her fingernails, long and sharp, glistened red; her skin glowed pale green and sickly. Two fangs protruded from her upper lip. She shrieked a laugh and struck out with her clawed hand towards the two white figures.

Dream Wil looked back at the white beast and the girl with the blue eyes. They were fading, growing more transparent.

He opened his mouth, but no words came. The girl smiled splendor and glory. She touched her hand to her forehead and down to her abdomen in an arc. "Farewell, Wil Johnson."

"Faded sight! Faded sight!" shrieked the banshee as she narrowed the distance between herself and Dream Wil. He worked his mouth, but dreamland gave him no voice to his thoughts. The two figures in white disappeared as the banshee grabbed at him.

Wil bolted up in his bed, perspiration dotting his face. He glanced around his room; gray morning filtered through his window. His alarm clock read 6:45 a.m. He wiped his face and got out of bed. Padding to the bathroom, he splashed cold water on his face and turned on the shower. As the water poured over him, he replayed the dream. Everything had seemed so vivid; that wasn't unusual. It was her, the girl. She seemed familiar somehow. What was it she had said?

"Do you know me, Wil Johnson? Can you still see?"

Still see what? And she had called him by name. She, the girl with the unicorn.

Wil washed the lather of soap from his body and turned off the water. He toweled off and brushed his teeth.

"Do you know me, Wil Johnson? Can you still see?"

The image of the unicorn flashed through Wil's mind. How

magnificent the creature had been, regal, powerful, pure. If only it was possible to *see* such a beast ...

Wil wiped his mouth and, wrapping the towel around himself, returned to his room to get dressed. Spring morning glowed against his window. He donned a pair of blue jeans and his favorite t-shirt.

"Can you still see?" The question nagged at him as he put on his socks and tied his shoes. *"Can you still see?"*

After slipping on his baseball cap and picking up his bookbag, he headed downstairs. Scott sat at the kitchen bar, busily munching a strip of bacon. He looked a little pale, as though he hadn't slept much.

"Morning, honey," Mrs. Johnson greeted Wil and handed him a plate. She gave him a second look. "You feeling okay?"

"Yeah. I just I had a weird dream, that's all."

Scott eyed him as he sat down. With a glance towards Mrs. Johnson, Scott said in a low voice, "Let me guess. Leprechaun World was invaded by a swarm of pixies."

"Don't be a jerk, Jerk." Wil spread jam on his toast.

Scott shook a warning finger at his friend. "That is why you need some bathing beauties in your room. Me? I had a wonderful dream last night, involving Nina Selna, a bikini, some water ..."

"Don't mind him, Mom," Wil said quickly as Mrs. Johnson cast an amused eye their way. "He's just a little dehydrated."

Scott nodded his head pointedly at Wil. His gray eyes glittered with mischief. "You could do a lot worse than Nina Selna. Oh, that's right. You have."

"Eat your eggs," Wil ordered.

"Wil, honey, I'm gonna be late tonight. They're having a meeting with all the potential candidates for Teresa's job, so I'm gonna leave you some money, and you can order some pizza."

"Mom's applying for a position that's come open," Wil explained to his friend.

"Oh, yeah?" Scott asked with interest. "I'll keep my fingers crossed for you, Mrs. J."

"Thanks, Scott. You two better hurry up, or you're gonna be late. Here's lunch for both of you."

Scott's eyes lit up. "Thanks, Mrs. J. Who do I need to call at work to tell 'em to give that job to you?"

She laughed. "You just concentrate on passing this year. The job will take care of itself." She kissed Wil on the head. "Have a good day."

"Thanks, Mom. And good luck!" he called as she picked up her keys and left the house. "Come on, we're gonna miss the bus."

After rinsing their plates, the two friends headed for the bus stop.

THE MORNING PASSED IN RELATIVE quiet. Wil had passed the pop quiz in science and had worked with Chris to complete the power point project due in history. Although he had seemed in good spirits most of the morning, the dream from the night before had lingered. Something, some untapped memory, pulled at the recesses of his mind.

"Can you still see?"

He wanted to, but he wasn't sure what he was supposed to be seeing.

Lunch time rolled around. Wil stood by the microwave, waiting for his cinnamon apples to heat up. After the microwave beeped, he took his bowl and his lunch bag to the table where his friends sat, busily eating.

"Oh, man," Scott said, chewing a mouthful of buttered noodles, "your mom is the best cook ever! I need to spend the night with you more often."

Wil eyed his friend cautiously. Old Scott seemed to be regaining control.

"That's all that poor woman needs: a house full of Scott." Stacey Jo shook her head.

"Don't be jealous, my pretty. I can still make time for you." Scott gave her an exaggerated wink.

Yep, Old Scott had made a full recovery.

"Yuck!" Stacey Jo shivered dramatically, then turned her back on him.

Wil stirred the cinnamon apples, the sweet, tangy odor tickling his nose.

"Can you still see?"

"Hey, Wil," Laurie interrupted his thoughts. "Derek and I are going to see the new Narnia movie this weekend. Do you want to go?"

"Prince Caspian? Yeah, that'd be great. Anybody else going?"

"Can't," Chris spoke up. "My dad's taking me fishing."

Stacey Jo shook her head. "I'm going to my grandma's. We're going to pick strawberries."

"Now *that* sounds like a good time," Scott jibed. Stacey Jo stuck her tongue out at him.

"Janet?"

She shook her curls. "I'm chaperoning my little sister's field trip to the museum. Her social studies class has been studying the prehistoric time period. She's psyched about going."

"That's cool," Chris commented as Wil took a bite of the cinnamon apples.

"Can you still see?"

Suddenly, the girl from Wil's dream pushed forward to the front of his mind. He stopped eating and stared inward, seeing her standing before him, her white gown fluttering in the gentle breeze, her honey colored ponytail held by a white cord, her blue eyes twinkling crystal clear.

"Do you know me, Wil Johnson?"

He saw himself standing behind the school, talking to one who appeared almost as an angel, yet was not. She dissolved into a thin, wispy cloud and floated away, yet remained standing at the edge of his memory.

"Do you know me, Wil Johnson?"

"Yes."

"Yes what?"

Wil looked up, not realizing he had spoken out loud. Scott stared at him, expectantly.

"Um, yes, it's cool that Janet's little sister is into cavemen and dinosaurs. Look, I need to go." Wil hurried through his words and the repacking of his lunch.

"Where?"

"The library. I'll see you in English class." He hurried away before his friends could question him further.

Scott shook his head. "The library?"

"It's a place with books, where people study," Stacey Jo said helpfully. "You wouldn't know of such a place."

Wil hurriedly signed in with the librarian and rushed to a computer. He logged on to a web site to search for names and typed in "Cassia."

Origin—Greek; meaning—Cinnamon, or from the spice tree. Cinnamon.

Wil's pulse quickened. Cinnamon.

"Class, this is Cassia Cloud."

Cassia. Cinnamon.

Wil sat back from the computer. His dream may have been just that, but the girl ... she was real. The girl with the unicorn.

"Do you know me, Wil Johnson? Can you still see?"

What it all meant, Wil didn't know. Why it was happening, he didn't know, either. What he did know was she was real, and it was enough to make him smile.

The bell ending lunch rang. Wil logged off the computer and picked up his bookbag. He strolled to English class, lost in thought. He remembered with sudden clarity the meeting behind the school. He was all too aware now of the scent of cinnamon and apples, a scent which seemed to be following him as he maneuvered through the throng of students.

He entered the classroom two steps behind Scott and Derek. Scott plopped into his desk, then gave his friend a look.

"The library? During lunch? Dude, that's like the only free time of the day. What gives?"

Wil shrugged and set his bookbag down. "I just had to look something up, that's all."

"And it couldn't have waited until you got home? What was it? The winning lottery combination?"

"No. Just something I thought about during lunch." Wil sat down, keeping his information a secret. He recalled the skepticism of his friends the first time he had tried to explain Cassia (his heart pulsed a little faster at the thought of her), not that he blamed them. He knew he sounded like a lunatic.

Stacey Jo and Laurie giggled their way into the classroom. Behind them skulked Andrew. Wil gave the boy a momentary glance; Andrew slouched to his seat, his face momentarily relaxed from its normal scowl. He seemed almost thoughtful, his gaze steady on something, or someone.

Wil allowed himself to casually follow the line of Andrew's gaze. It came to rest on the girl sitting in the desk beside Scott. It came to rest on Laurie.

Wil started in surprise. He tapped Scott on the shoulder and gave a subtle glance in Andrew's direction. Scott followed Wil's look, then followed Andrew's. He, too, started in surprise before disgust settled on his face. Before either boy could say anything, however, Ms. Frank tapped on her desk to bring the class to order. The bell rang, and Ms. Frank turned on the overhead projector.

"Good afternoon, class. Today, we will be studying mythology. Can anyone tell me what a myth is?"

Laurie raised her hand.

"Yes, Laurie?"

"I think it's a type of story that tries to explain how something was created in nature, like flowers or trees."

Ms. Frank smiled. "Very good, Laurie."

Laurie smiled and shrugged playfully at Derek. Wil pretended to scratch his chin on his shoulder on the pretense of stealing another glance at Andrew. A small smile played on Andrew's lips as he watched Laurie's red ponytail swing from side to side as she shifted in her seat.

Wil stared a little longer than he should have. He couldn't help himself. He had never seen Andrew show any sort of gentility, and it was just too incredible that Andrew could be that interested in anyone, let alone one of Wil's friends. However, he mistimed his gaze, and Andrew caught him staring. Immediately, the all-too-familiar scowl settled onto his face, and he balled up one fist while Ms. Frank's attention was diverted to the overhead.

Wil turned back around in his seat and slouched just a tad. He picked up his pen and began copying down the notes. Just then, the door opened and in floated Cassia.

Wil started up, his heart hammering so loud he was sure Scott and Derek could hear it.

"My apologies at my tardiness, Ms. Frank," Cassia said politely. Her voice sounded musical, like a harp. Her eyes drifted out to the students and settled on Wil. He seemed sucked into the depths of those blue spheres which bore right into him.

"Do you know me, Wil Johnson?"

The question echoed in his mind, and he nodded involuntarily.

Ms. Frank took the note and perused it quickly. "No problem. We are just beginning our discussion on mythology. I believe your name is of Greek origin, isn't it? That should fit in well with our lesson. You may take your seat."

Cassia smiled warmly at Ms. Frank, and Wil felt a twinge of envy that such glory should be directed towards anyone else.

Scott took the opportunity to lean up and tap Laurie on the shoulder.

"Did you know Andrew's staring at you?"

Laurie stared at Scott for about three seconds, then stole a glance to the back of the room. Andrew averted his gaze as soon as she looked his way, only to let his eyes drift back her way as though he was looking at everyone in the room. She gave him a small smile; Andrew blinked, a half smile pulling at his mouth. He quickly looked down at his hands as though he was shy.

Laurie glanced back at Scott. "So?"

"So? *So? So?* That is Andrew McGhee! You seriously cannot be crushing on him!"

"I didn't say anything about crushing on him, but I don't hate him, either."

Scott opened his mouth to respond, but Ms. Frank had turned back to the overhead. Cassia moved towards her seat. Her blue eyes twinkled, and a small smile played on her lips, as though she knew she had won some victory that no one else knew about.

Wil watched her as she floated to her desk and sat down. Great radiance surrounded her, bathing her in brilliant light.

"Wow," he heard Scott whisper. Wil shot him a look. Surely Scott had to see it now. His friend met his gaze and shrugged in innocent protest.

Wil glanced around the room; the boys were staring at Cassia, open admiration still evident on their faces. All except Andrew, who stared at her, his face crinkled up in a scowl. *Figures*, Wil thought, turning his attention back to the lesson at hand; he was now resigned to the fact that, for whatever reason, he alone was witness to this oddity.

"Gentlemen," Ms. Frank called out suddenly, "while I am sure Cassia appreciates your attentions, I would appreciate your focusing a little more on the lesson up front."

Cassia glanced around. She smiled at the boys who were shamelessly ogling her. Her gaze lingered a moment on Andrew who, like Wil, avoided her gaze. When she turned back to the front, she had a thoughtful expression on her calm face.

Wil forced himself to focus on the lesson. He picked up his pen and wrote down a word, then glanced at her. She smiled at him and turned her attention back to Ms. Frank.

This afternoon, Wil Johnson. We will talk then.

He jumped and knocked his book into the floor.

"Smooth," Scott murmured. Wil ignored him and picked up the book. He looked to Cassia for an explanation, but she now ignored him. She didn't look his way again until the bell ending class rang.

Cassia stood and glanced meaningfully at Wil before sailing out of the room. Wil was certain her feet had not touched the floor, but he didn't hesitate to ponder it. He scooped all of his books into his bag and bolted from the room.

Straining to see over the tops of his peers' heads, he spotted her several paces ahead of him. It wasn't too difficult to see her; she glowed with an ethereal light that was lovely against the stark plainness of the walls and lockers.

Wil followed her outside and down to the football stadium. He longed to ask her a zillion questions, but her silence told him to be patient. Only once they were safely hidden underneath the bleachers did she speak.

"Greetings, Wil Johnson."

"Cassia." He tested the name out loud. She smiled and tilted her head in a small bow. "Wow. You are really real. I wasn't sure. I mean," he rambled on, unable to stop himself, "I had this dream and you were in it, only I thought it was just a dream. But it wasn't. It was real."

"Yes."

Wil inhaled sharply. "Then that means the unicorn ... there was one in my dream. That was real, too, right?"

She smiled. "He is as real as you need him to be."

Wil puzzled over her response, but a thousand other questions assailed his mind. "What does this mean? How is it I know you? How is it you know me? What are you? Where did you come from?"

She found his enthusiasm amusing. "I come from a realm far above your earth."

"But you're not an angel."

"No. Heaven is that realm which exists far above *us*. We exist on a sphere separating Heaven from Earth."

"We? So there're more of you?"

"Oh, yes. We exist among those." She pointed to the blue sky; singular clouds drifted lazily in an array of patterns.

"Clouds?" Wil stared incredulously at her. "You're a what? Cloud person?"

She shrugged. "That is as good a title as any, I suppose. We exist on that realm which carries the clouds you see every day. We are of their substance; that is our true existence."

To prove her point, she waved her hand; it faded into a thin wispy mist that trailed up her arm to her shoulder. Then, just as suddenly, her arm and hand reappeared, solid and fleshy.

Wil gaped, shook his head in disbelief, and stared again.

"But you're able to be in human form whenever you want?"

"Yes. We have been studying mankind since the sun first rose out of the heavens. It took many moons before we developed the ability to appear as one of you, but that ability was born out of necessity. We needed to maintain the Balance at all costs." She paused. "It is actually quite thrilling to be in human form." She wiggled her fingers. "Interesting protrusions, these."

Wil studied her, sure he had lost all sanity. "So, why are you here?"

"I am here for you, Wil Johnson. That is all you need to know now. To tell you more would be…" she searched for the right word, "overwhelming."

"Okay. I'm not sure I understand what that means. I mean, this whole thing is kind of overwhelming. Besides, you wouldn't believe how many questions I have."

"And they will all be answered in due time." She glanced skyward. "Well, I must go now. It is time."

"Wait!" Wil cried, startling Cassia. "Sorry." He glanced down at his shoes meekly. When he met her eyes again, he had regained a little composure. "Will I see you again?"

She beamed at him. "Of course. We have much to discuss."

He looked relieved at her words. "Just one more thing. My friends … they don't see you the same way I do. I mean, you glow. At least, that's what I see when I look at you. They don't. Why?"

Radiance glowed all around her; she seemed pleased with the question. "Because, Wil Johnson, you believe."

With that, she shimmered into a milky white cloud, wispy and thin, and floated towards the heavens.

Chapter 4

"Okay, so what happened to you today?" Scott asked. "You took off like a rocket after English. Thanks, by the way, for the extra laps at practice."

"I had something to do," Wil responded vaguely. The two friends sat outside underneath a bright orange sun sinking in the west. The late afternoon heat warmed their arms as they lounged in the patio chairs, a half-empty pizza box between them.

"That clears it up. Thanks."

Wil ignored the sarcasm in Scott's voice. Instead, he focused on the pumpkin colored clouds overhead.

"What do you think about those clouds?" he asked suddenly.

"What?" Scott glanced overhead, then back at his friend.

"Do you think it's possible that they're magical?"

"Not that again. Dude, they're clouds." Scott rolled his eyes in disgust and plopped back in his chair. "You know, evaporated water. Nothing magical about it. I mean, if you want to talk magic, let's talk about Cassia. She's got a spell cast on everybody in class."

"Cassia?" Wil looked at him, his pulse quickening at the thought of her. "What do you mean?"

"Um, don't tell me you didn't notice her?"

"Of course I noticed her. It was hard not to."

Scott feigned relief. "Thank goodness! I was beginning to

worry about you." He paused and glanced slyly at his friend. "She is pretty, isn't she?"

"Yeah, she is." An image of crystal blue eyes filled Wil's mind. He became aware of Scott's silence and blinked himself back to reality. Scott grinned at him. Wil shrugged to cover his embarrassment. "But so what? There are lots of pretty girls at school."

"Yes, but none of them have ever gotten your attention. Not like this one. And that's where I think you were this afternoon. Is it?"

"No."

"It is, too!"

"So what? I just went to … welcome her to school and to make sure she wasn't upset by all the staring that *some* people did."

"Hey, I can't help it if I have an appreciation for beauty." Scott took a slice of pizza from the box. "I'm just happy you seem to be finally coming around."

"It's not like that."

"Well, it should be."

Wil shook his head and looked back at the heavens. The clouds were outlined by the setting sun. He wondered which one belonged to Cassia and when he would see her again. He hoped it wouldn't be too long.

It wasn't.

Though he looked for her at first waking and all the way to school, it wasn't until science class that he saw her again. Today, once he got past the glow, he noticed she wore a skirt the color of freshly grown grass and a deep yellow blouse with sheered sleeves.

He also noticed that, once again, all the boys in class seemed mesmerized by Cassia, although he was quite certain they didn't see the radiance that he saw. Even Juan Archuro seemed quite awake and attentive. When Mr. Golden suggested Cassia sit at his table, Juan beamed and hurriedly cleared his books out of the way.

Wil's eyes followed her to her seat. As she sat, she glanced his way and smiled at him.

"Today, my little Edisons, we will be discussing the properties of rocks." Mr. Golden ignored the groans from the class and turned on the projector. "Please take your notes as usual as you will need them for the lab assignment during the second half of class."

As he started the power point presentation, Wil stole a peek at Cassia. He blinked in surprise before forcing himself not to be too amazed, at least not after what had happened yesterday: Though it seemed that she was removing pen and paper from the satchel she had slung over a shoulder, Wil was certain that she had conjured them from thin air. When she placed the tip of the pen against the paper, it seemed as though she copied the notes, yet Wil was certain that the pen tip never moved from its original spot. When she lifted the pen, however, the words drifted from the space around her and landed on the page.

Janet elbowed him and pointed towards the overhead screen. Wil realized he had missed the first few slides and quickly began copying the notes. It seemed to him that the note-taking went on forever; he was impatient to speak to Cassia, to ask her more questions, to learn more about who she was and why she was here. Finally, Mr. Golden switched off the projector and flipped on the lights.

"Now, then, today we will be testing your powers of observation," he instructed. "If you will please take notice, at each of your lab stations there is a box. Inside each box are six different rocks. You are to identify each rock according to its properties. Then, tonight for homework, you will use your notes to compose a two-page paper in which you compare and contrast the six rocks used into today's lessons." Another collective groan from the class. "Oh, and by the way, each station has different rocks, so no trying to cheat from station to station. You may get started."

The students rose from their seats and moved to their stations. Mr. Golden moved from one lab to the next, assisting the students as they worked. Wil watched with some disappointment as Cassia joined Juan, Cindy, and Brian at station three. He had hoped she would join him at station five so he could talk to her. As such, he had trouble concentrating on his task.

"Wil!" Janet called, waving her hand in front of his face. He blinked and looked at her. "You're not doing your part."

He looked at his three lab partners. "Sorry. I'm just a little unfocused this morning."

"Yeah, well, get focused," Janet scolded. "We don't have but thirty minutes left in class, and we still have four rocks to go through."

"Right." Wil wrote down some notes, forcing himself not to look at or think about Cassia.

Patience, Wil Johnson. Her gentle voice filled his head and relaxed him. *We will talk soon.*

He glanced at her. She smiled at him. Wil smiled back and returned to his work with renewed vigor.

WIL FOUND CASSIA WAITING FOR him by his locker right before lunch. Her presence made his stomach flip-flop.

"Greetings, Wil Johnson."

"Hi." He fumbled with his lock to cover his nervousness. "How did you like science class?"

"I enjoyed it very much. Humans study very interesting things. We have nothing like rocks where I come from."

Wil popped open the lock and removed it so he could open his locker. He changed out books. "There are more interesting things to study, I assure you." He slammed his locker shut and replaced the lock as Scott and Chris joined them.

"Oh, man, that was so classic!" Chris laughed. He stopped when he saw Cassia. His expression changed to one of open admiration. "Hi. I'm ... I'm Chris Cates."

Cassia smiled at him. "Hello, Chris Cates. I'm Cassia."

"Oh, you're the one everybody's talking about. Well, I will say that for once, Scott didn't exaggerate."

Cassia drew a puzzled look at the three boys. Scott wiggled his fingers at her and made a formal bow.

"I'm Scott, a huge admirer of yours. I must say, you brighten up these dingy hallways, and for that, I am grateful."

Cassia gazed at him a moment longer, as if seeing something the others couldn't see.

"Cut it out," Wil chastised. Their admiration of her made him uncomfortable. He tried to change their focus. "What were you talking about? What was so classic?"

Chris seemed to snap out of his reverie. "Oh, Scott pulled a fast one on Mr. Lou's substitute this morning. It was great. I'm not even sure he's figured it out yet. The whole class was rolling."

"Thank you, thank you," Scott replied as they made their way towards the cafeteria. "Just another talent I was blessed with." He paused as they neared the doorway. "Ooh, I smell spaghetti!"

"Hey, there's Stacey Jo and Janet already," Chris said as they headed for their table.

"What is this place?" Cassia asked Wil, who hung back a little from his friends.

"It's called a cafeteria. It's where we get our food."

She seemed thoughtful for a moment. "Oh, yes. Food. It is that sustenance which you need to exist, yes?"

He stared at her for a moment, sorting out what she said. "Yeah. I guess you don't eat in the clouds."

She smiled at him and shook her head.

"Oh, well, come on. I'll introduce you to my other friends." He sat down. "Hey, guys. This is Cassia. Cassia, this is Janet and Stacey Jo, Laurie and Derek. You just met Chris and Scott."

"Oh, you met Scott?" Stacey Jo asked in horror. "We're really sorry about him. There's just nothing to be done. He is the way he is, and we have had to learn to deal with it."

Cassia looked to Wil for an explanation of what Stacey Jo was talking about, but Wil just waved her off with a "never-mind" gesture.

"So, how do you like it here?" Janet asked, sprinkling pepper on her potatoes.

"I like it very much." Cassia's enthusiasm was very nearly contagious. "There is so much to see and learn."

"Really?" Stacey Jo seemed skeptical. "Is it really that much different where you're from?"

Cassia exchanged a look with Wil before replying, "Oh, yes, it is really that much different."

A lone figure sitting across the cafeteria caught her attention. She pointed him out to Wil.

"Why is that boy sitting by himself?"

Wil looked up. He frowned. "That's Andrew McGhee. *That's* why he's sitting alone."

"I do not follow you."

"He's not a very nice person."

"Who?" asked Chris as he and Scott joined them, trays in hands.

"Andrew."

Scott scowled. "He's a punk. He's gonna pick on the wrong person on the wrong day and get what's coming to him."

Cassia blinked. The sensation flowing from the kids seated around her was new and different and strange. She focused on Scott again. Her brow furrowed as she tried to connect the sensations with what she saw. The other kids continued their chatter, unaware of her scrutiny.

"Oh, I don't know," Laurie piped up. "I don't think he's so bad."

Derek scowled. "He's a jerk! You know he's always bullying people."

"So? He's kind of cute, in a bad boy sort of way."

"You are so totally crushing on him!" Scott accused.

"I am not!" Laurie went pink in the face. "But I don't want to be any part of the 'I-hate-Andrew' club, either."

"Girls," Derek muttered and received a dirty look from Stacey Jo.

Cassia studied Andrew from across the room. There was something familiar about him. He stared into space, seemingly oblivious to everyone around him. After a moment, his eyes lighted on her, seated among Wil and his friends. His eyes crinkled in puzzlement as though he wasn't sure exactly what it was he was seeing. He stood suddenly, a look of concern flitting across his face, and hurried out of the cafeteria.

Cassia sat in thoughtful silence. The sensation ebbing from the kids had faded as they discussed other matters.

"Hey, are you okay?" Wil asked in a low voice.

"Of course." She smiled at him. "We will talk at the setting of the sun. There is much I need to tell you."

WIL SAT ON HIS BED later that evening. Evening sounds drifted up to his open second story window: children playing in the street, a twilight bird twittering good-night, the occasional car passing. He watched the sky grow darker and darker. Warm air pushed itself into his room along with the scent of magnolia blossoms.

He sighed and turned back towards his essay for science. He had completed one page so far, a half-hearted attempt that would do little to increase his C-minus average. He wrote two sentences, erased one, wrote two more, then erased all three before tossing his notebook aside. He sighed and dropped his head back onto his headboard.

Just before he saw her, he caught the scent of cinnamon apples. He sat up in anticipation as a thin mist flowed through his open window and transformed into the familiar form of Cassia. She blinked and looked around, her white gown a brilliant spot in his darkening room.

"Greetings, Wil Johnson." She smiled gloriously at him.

"I … wasn't sure you were coming," Wil admitted after a moment.

"I said I would come." She seemed puzzled by his doubt.

"I know, it's just that…" he gestured to the darkening sky. "Well, it's getting late, and then I didn't see you this afternoon." He paused. "Why weren't you in class?"

"I had some…" she searched for the right word, "ideas on which I had to ponder. Meditation is a vital part of our existence, especially when something perplexes us."

"What is it?"

She hesitated, considering. "I am not here to burden you with my questions, Wil Johnson. I am here to answer some of yours."

"Oh." Wil sat very still for a moment. He had a thousand questions, but he wasn't sure where to begin. "Okay. Um…" He looked up. She stood, waiting patiently, her blue eyes focused solely on him. He felt pulled towards them and cut his gaze short. Standing, he pretended an interest in one of the dragon figurines on his night stand.

"Um, before, when we talked, you said that you, your people assumed human form in order to maintain the Balance. What did that mean?"

She stepped further into the room, the white cord wrapped around her ponytail gleaming brightly from some unknown light source.

"Yes, that must be explained." She inhaled deeply; the sweet scent of cinnamon swirled around Wil's room. When she looked at him, her eyes gleamed, the color of sapphires. "The Balance consists of equal parts good and evil. It is those forces which drive the very nature of your planet: what is right and what is wrong. You know of this, yes?"

"Of course." Wil set the figurine down. "That's what we learn when we're little. But what have your people got to do with it?"

"*We* are the Balance." Cassia watched him closely.

"I don't understand."

"No, but you will. You must." She eyed the open window. "Can you guard the night from seeing?"

"Huh?" Wil glanced at the window, interpreted her words without really knowing how, and reached over to let the blinds down. "Better?"

She nodded. "Come closer, Wil Johnson. There is something you must see."

Wil moved around the edge of his bed, eyeing her cautiously. She waved her hand. A glowing orb of light appeared out of thin air and hovered over them. Wil's eyes widened in amazement as she reached up and scooped the orb into her hand. Bringing it to eye level, she instructed him, "See the past, Wil Johnson."

Wil gazed into the orb. The brilliant light faded away until only a soft, moonlight glow emitted from it. Inside the sphere, clouded images appeared, muted and milky at first. As he watched, the images began to take on form, and Cassia narrated for him:

"Many thousands of moons ago, when the first cloud appeared in the great heavens, there rode upon it a mighty power. This power flowed across the skies, absorbing all knowledge of life blossoming on this planet below. The more knowledge the power gained, the easier it was for this power to assume a shape, a form not unlike that of the cloud upon which it resided. This form pulled pieces of life from all that it witnessed and eventually created more clouds to fill the great heavens, and from those clouds this form created others like itself. As other forms were created, so too were other clouds and more forms and more clouds until the vastness of the sky was filled with a plethora of life.

"The original form became known as Olin, father of my people. He took his knowledge of this world and that from which we were created and schooled his children in the art of observation. Olin knew no malice and did not pass on such to his children. Rather, he passed on gentleness and respect for all life forms. As the moons passed, newer life appeared on this planet, and with the coming of each new species, Olin and his children studied and learned all they could, for he had prophecied the coming of a species with which communication would one day be possible. Olin believed that would be the key to bridging the gap between this world and his; he longed to give the species of this planet the knowledge that he and his children had acquired over the many phases of the moons, for it was not just an astuteness of the brain which Olin's children held, but a knowledge of the elements, of the trees, of the sea itself."

"Magic," Wil breathed, watching the images dance across the orb.

"Yes," she smiled. "Magic, only there was no species which Olin felt could understand its depths. So he waited, and his children waited with him, until such a time as man first walked on this planet. It was in man whom Olin recognized the ability to reason, the ability to understand and learn and adapt. So it was to man Olin bestowed the acumen of enchantment and the supernatural.

"During this time, great peace reigned over this world, for Olin had blessed the human inhabitants with such fortune. But man began to become slovenly, selfish. He no longer appreciated the beauty of the trees or the warmth of the sun; he began to complain when it was too wet or too cold, when the ground was too hard for planting or when he was called to aid his neighbor. Olin's children tried, but they had no means of communicating with the humans. Understanding of what was happening did not come easily to my people. Only Olin noticed, he being the keen observer that he was. A malice that was both dark and strong had been born out of man's use of fire. It was very subtle at first, a puff of smoke, a flicker of blue flame. But this malice had determined itself to live, to take on a form of power that was much greater than the light and heat established by the fire flames.

"It took many moons, but the malice succeeded, as had Olin, in taking shape. This form slipped into the crevices of the planet where the molten rivers flow, ash, soot, lava rock. And there, this form pulled life from the ashes to create more forms like it. The difference was these forms did not study the planet to learn from it; they studied to find its weaknesses. Olin believes that the smoky soot burned away any conscience the new life form had. So up from the core rose Meslo and his children. Wherever they laid hand or foot, ill will fell.

"Man's strength had weakened during this time of sloth and selfishness. Meslo's children did not have to try too hard to poison one against another. As Olin and his children watched from above, the venom that was Meslo's spread, and man began to turn against his neighbor, his planet, and himself. Olin called his children together; he had foreseen the destruction of the planet that he had come to love, and he knew man could not withstand the forces of malice by himself. That is when Olin met Meslo over the great plains. It was a clash the world has not seen since. The father of the clouds battled the father of the fires for many moons. Light battled darkness, love battled malice, all in the sky, on the sea, and upon the crevices of the earth.

"Olin's children blew their breath upon the humans; some recovered from their bouts of cruelty and joined the fight, spreading love and peace. Others succumbed to the rigors of hate and fought for the other side. Creatures fled into hiding, the trees pulled into themselves, the seas seemed to dry up. And then, when all hope had appeared to vanish and your Earth was at its darkest, Olin managed to maim Meslo. With the Fire King defeated, Olin's children were able to push the figures of malevolence down into the core of the planet and seal them inside forever. Thus, the Great Battle ended, and Olin had grown a little wiser for it.

"You see, during the Great Battle, Olin had an epiphany: the fighting existed because he and Meslo were opposites. One was good, the other evil. Man would submit either way, either due to weakness or great understanding. Once the fighting ceased, many humans returned to the old ways of hard work and discipline, of aiding one another and seeking higher knowledge. Some humans continued on the path set forth by Meslo. But what was important was the realization that this world had righted itself somehow, and now the energies flowing up from the planet seemed stable. That is when Olin understood that his people and Meslo's people existed for a single reason: to maintain the existence of the other." Here the orb went dark, erasing all images from Wil's eyes. Cassia waved her hand and the lifeless ball vanished.

"It is at this point that the Balance was established and kept in check for all these many moons by my people. Olin recognized that good cannot exist without evil, that if the humans of this planet were going to appreciate the benevolence in this world, they were going to have to be made aware of the calamity that existed as well."

She paused. Wil stared at the spot where the orb had been. His head whirled with all of this information. He rubbed his eyes and when he opened them, he spotted his notebook lying on the floor. To think, just a few short hours ago, he had been concerned about a paper on the properties of rocks!

"So, then, all of that stuff about the forces of good and evil, it's all true." He sat down on the edge of the bed. He seemed disappointed, though he didn't know why; he never expected it to be any other way. If there was no evil, no malice, then his dad wouldn't be dead, Scott's dad wouldn't be a drunk, Andrew wouldn't be a bully. Still, he couldn't deny that he had hoped she would tell him differently; after all, if one dream becomes a reality, is it too much to expect other dreams to become real also?

"Yes."

"And your people guard the Balance … protect it. From what?"

She sat down beside him. Her nearness warmed Wil. He felt strange and light; if she told him the world was ending tomorrow, he doubt he would have cared.

"From the animosity that still exists. The Balance cannot tip either way."

Wil shook his head. "But wouldn't it be better to strengthen the good, to lessen the amount of evil in the world? Why does it have to exist?" He looked into her face and felt his breath come short. Her skin had a lovely ivory tint to it in the glow of his lamp, and her eyes had converted back to crystal blue.

She smiled gently at him. "How would you know something is good if you have nothing by which to judge it?"

Wil shook his head, his eyes lighting on the picture of his mom and dad on vacation.

As if sensing his weariness, Cassia stood. "And now, Wil Johnson, I will bid you farewell. I have given you much to think about, and I believe the time for your meditation has arrived."

Wil glanced at his window. The blind was mysteriously up, and a large yellow moon gazed down at the sleeping neighborhood. He was surprised by the lateness of the hour. "Will you be in school tomorrow?"

"Of course. I am only just beginning in my tasks. Rest well, Wil Johnson, and do not worry about all I told you. It will make sense in time." She touched her hand to her forehead, then to her abdomen in a small arc. "Til we meet again." Then she faded into a wispy mist and drifted out of his window into the night.

Chapter 5

Wil met Cassia at his locker the next morning. She smiled at him, the pink in her shirt complimenting the natural blush in her cheeks.

"Greetings, Wil Johnson. Did you have a pleasant meditation last night?"

"Yes, I slept very well. And you know, you can just call me 'Wil.' You don't have to say my whole name every time you see me."

"I have noticed that humans do that, call each other by only one name. Why, then, do you have two names?"

Wil paused in filling his bookbag. "I don't know. I guess because there are so many of us, we use two names to identify ourselves. You know," he shut his locker and they started down the hall, "in case there's more than one 'Wil' in a class. The teacher would call me 'Wil Johnson' or 'Wil J.' to avoid confusion."

"So there are other people like you named Wil?" She seemed amazed at the thought.

"Yes. Well, no, not other *me's*, but there are other people named Wil and Scott and Laurie." He stopped walking and looked at her. "Don't you have other Cassia's where you're from?"

"No. I am the only one with that name."

"But didn't you say that there were thousands of ..." he glanced around and whispered the next word, "cloud people up there?"

"Yes, but just as each cloud is different and unique, so, too, are Olin's children. He named each of us himself, and no two children have the same name."

A couple of students at their lockers gave Wil and Cassia odd looks. Wil smiled and started to steer Cassia down the hall. However, something had her attention. He glanced over his shoulder; several feet away stood Andrew. He watched them unabashedly. Inwardly, Wil groaned.

"You do not care for him," Cassia observed. "Why?"

"He's a whole lot of trouble," Wil responded. It was hard to keep his voice neutral.

"What does that mean, 'a whole lot of trouble'?"

"Nothing." She looked at him, her eyes dark and intense. Wil relented.

"Look, remember when you told me last night that some of Meslo's influence lasted even after the Great Battle was over?" She nodded. "Well, let's just say that Andrew is one of those that could very easily be swayed to his side."

The bell for the first class rang.

"Come on," Wil said, shifting his bookbag. "Let's get to class."

Cassia considered his words for a moment. She glanced back at Andrew, only he was no longer there. Something felt wrong; she just couldn't sort it out. However, when Wil turned and waited for her, she pushed the feeling aside. She followed Wil (although he was convinced she floated) to class.

SCHOOL PROVED TO BE MUCH more interesting with Cassia. Wil noticed that the habitually sleepy Juan Archuro had found enough reason to stay awake in science class. From his lab station, Wil watched as Cassia listened with interest to something being explained to her by Juan. Juan reached into his jacket pocket and pulled out a starfish, which he showed to Cassia. Her face lit with pleasure at seeing it. Juan passed it to her, and Cassia held the starfish in the palm of her hand. Wil was certain he saw the starfish's rays bend and move. Cassia smiled at Juan as she passed it back to him; Wil noticed the boy's cheeks flush pink and go deeper red when Mr. Golden praised their lab results.

During his second period class, history, Wil noticed Cassia hovering near the window. She sat with her legs crossed, her attention focused on Mr. Alps as he explained the significance of the stock market crash of 1929. Behind her, through the window, Wil saw ghosts from the past: men holding up signs for work, women and children standing in a bread line, farmers struggling against great dust clouds.

Wil met Cassia's eyes. She merely smiled at him and turned her attention towards the front board. Wil shook his head and picked up his pen as the ghosts drifted away on a gentle breeze.

However, it was during lunch that something happened which intrigued Wil the most. He and his friends sat in their usual spot. Cassia was not with them; Wil had not been able to find her after second period. She had slipped through the window just before the bell rang and had not reappeared.

Wil listened to his friends' chatter without much participation, instead keeping his eyes wide open for any sign of Cassia.

"Seriously, though, Nikki gets on my nerves," Stacey Jo complained. "She's not even our captain, but she's always giving us orders. She wants to be the top of the pyramid, but we keep telling her she's got to lay off the cookies. Like we could haul her elephant butt up there."

"That's not very nice," Laurie scolded, though she giggled.

"I'm not saying it to be mean," Stacey Jo defended herself. "But there's a reason Nina's got her on the bottom."

"So, you see, if you multiply the variables here," Janet explained to Derek, "this becomes the negative, which makes *this* the answer."

"Oh, god, you're a genius," Derek sighed. "Maybe you should teach our class. At least then some of us might actually pass."

"I know. Who hired Ms. Allbright?" Chris asked, opening his thermos. "She never explains anything. It's like we get ten minutes out of the whole class to actually focus on the objective of the day. The rest of the time, she's going over our homework."

"That could be helpful," Janet replied.

Derek and Chris gawked at her.

"For a whole hour?" Derek demanded. "I don't think so."

"It can't be that bad."

"Stop by sometime," Chris challenged.

Wil scanned the cafeteria again. No sign of Cassia. It was then that he became aware of an unusual silence. He looked over at Scott. No food sat in front of his friend, and an unnatural scowl was just evident between his eyes. Wil leaned in to his friend so their conversation wouldn't be heard by the others.

"You okay?"

"Yep."

"You're not eating?"

"No. My dad …" Scott chuckled bitterly. "He took the money out of my bag last night. Spent the night at Mackee's Bar."

"Well, here." Wil pushed half his sandwich towards Scott. "My mom always packs way too much." He pulled out a bag of pretzels, a banana, and bowl of grapes.

Scott shook his head. "I'm not that hungry."

Wil looked down at his lunch. He didn't know what to say; he didn't know how to deal with Quiet Scott. Feeling somewhat guilty, he began putting his food back into his bag. Just then, he spotted Cassia over Scott's shoulder. She stood in the doorway of the cafeteria, looking around. She spotted him and smiled. However, she didn't move to sit with him. Instead, she crossed the cafeteria to where a lone figure sat in the far corner of the room.

Wil gaped, and Scott turned around to see what had Wil's attention. Seeing where Cassia had gone, Scott let loose a low whistle and looked back at his friend.

"Guess I'm not the only one who's having a sucky moment."

Wil gave him a dirty look, then turned his attention across the room.

Cassia stood in front of Andrew. He looked up at her, momentarily startled. His shaggy black hair fell into his dark eyes, eyes that now puzzled over the girl standing at his table.

"Greetings," she said amicably.

"What do you want?"

"I wonder that you sit alone when there are so many people in this room, and that you do not have food. Why do you have no carrier in front of you?"

Andrew gaped at her. His eyes darted around the cafeteria; he saw Wil watching them, and a scowl settled on his face. He frowned up at Cassia.

"Look here, Sweets, I don't know what you and your little freaky friends are up to, but I'm only gonna tell you once: leave me the hell alone."

Cassia took a step back as new sensations, wild and violent, filled her. She forced them down and exhaled.

"I do not understand what you mean."

"I'm sure you don't."

Cassia considered him for a moment. He wasn't looking at her now. She sat down across from him.

"Why do you sit here alone?"

He looked up at her, his eyes blazing with anger and confusion. "What do you care? Are you the Goodwill Ambassador or something?"

"No. I am merely curious. I have observed that humans require constant contact with one another, yet you do not engage in social activities. Is there a reason?"

Andrew chuckled. "You've got to be kidding." He leaned forward, tossing the hair out of his eyes as he did so. "Look, it's real simple. I don't want to hang out with a bunch of losers. That's why I sit here by myself."

"Losers?"

"Yeah, losers." Andrew's gaze bore right into Cassia. "I don't need anybody. Not them, and not you." He stood up and walked away.

Cassia stared after him. She was overcome by an empty feeling; she felt completely devoid of emotion for several seconds. Then, when Andrew passed Wil's table, the wild, violent vibrations rushed at her, taking her breath away. She steadied herself with a few deep breaths. Looking over at Wil and his friends, she counted. Seven to one. Interesting, she mused. It seemed there were many dynamics regarding human behavior, dynamics that she couldn't make sense of. She was thankful to hear the bell ring; meditation would help her regain her composure.

Wil was the last one to leave the cafeteria. He watched Cassia, sitting with her head in her hand. He wanted to speak to her, to say something that might make her feel better, but all he could think of was "told you so," so he stayed put. After another minute, he turned and headed for his third period class.

CASSIA STOOD BEFORE THE COUNCIL. She felt calm and settled here among her own kind. The befuddling sensations she had felt earlier had all dissipated, and she felt prepared to give her report to those sitting before her.

"How goes your observation, Cassia?" Rebecca asked. Her blue eyes stood out greatly in the brilliant whiteness of the room.

"I believe it goes well. Wil Johnson has accepted the information regarding the Balance and the Great Battle. I believe he is ready to assume the responsibility of Secret Keeper."

"Agreed," replied Devlin, folding his hands on the table. "The Council has been quite pleased with the progress your Wil Johnson is making. He seems determined to hold onto his belief in magic. This will fare well for everyone."

"We do have a concern, however," Samson added. Cassia looked at him, making sure to keep her thoughts suppressed. "You have by now, no doubt, encountered some negative energy from these humans, those emotions to which we are not accustomed."

Cassia nodded.

Samson continued. "We are aware of the temporary break from this world you experienced earlier. There is cause for concern, do you not agree?"

"Do you mean that emptiness from earlier?"

"Yes," answered Rayle. "Those of us who have ventured to Earth have often experienced such sensations. It is a common reaction to their powerful emotions."

Clover spoke up. "You must be prepared to experience such moments until you become adjusted to their varying pathos."

"But understand," Samson continued, "it takes many moons to develop the ability to filter out such sensations. Humans are quite complex in their abilities to feel. Though you will become used to them in time, do not expect to understand them. I myself still do not understand their anger or ecstasy, though I have learned when to expect it."

Cassia nodded. She noticed Charlie watching her carefully and kept her gaze focused on the other council members.

"There is one other task you must undertake during your observation," Jereni said solemnly. "When seven moons have passed, you must go to this shelter." The large orb to Cassia's right blazed to life. A house came into view. Cassia studied it while Jereni continued.

"Something will happen at this location which will bring together forces to affect your Wil Johnson. Those forces will begin to appear tonight. You must be present when these events happen."

"How will they affect him?" Cassia felt their concern.

"That we cannot say." Rayle's gravelly voice drew her attention. "The complexity of the human prevents us from making an accurate observation. It is deeper than the tiger striking out of fear or hunger and nothing else."

"But you are concerned."

"Yes." Jereni leaned forward. "Wil Johnson may very well cast off his innocence after these events. If that happens, the truth of our people may be in jeopardy."

"If that happens," Ballari interrupted, "he becomes a very real target for Meslo's corruption."

"But," Samson added, "he may very well hold onto his innocence. You are to see that he does. That is why you must be present when these events unfold."

Cassia considered their words. Their concern was very real and very justified. "I understand."

"Good. Then we will reconvene at such a time as the course of this plan is determined," Samson declared. Cassia nodded solemnly at the Council before leaving the great hall. As she stepped out into the radiant blue of the sky realm, she felt Charlie approaching her. She waited for him, knowing what he would say.

"Cassia, you withheld information from the Council, did you not?" he asked, coming right to the point.

She kept her gaze steady. "No. I have no other information to report."

"You understand the point of the question."

"Yes, but none of my other observations have been confirmed. I will tell them when I have proof."

Charlie sighed. "This is precarious, at best. The consequences ... "

"Are the same as they were when Wil Johnson's trust was in question." Cassia shook her head. "I do not feel any threat to us. We cannot change what may not be."

Charlie did not seem pleased with this, but he could not argue with her logic. "I urge you find the truth as soon as you can. Our secret must be kept at all costs."

"I understand." She gave him an encouraging smile. "Farewell, Charlie. Until we meet again." After making the familiar gesture, she slipped through the clouds and drifted down towards the earth.

THAT NIGHT, WIL LOUNGED ON the couch. He flipped through the TV stations, bored. He wished Cassia would return. He had many more things he wanted to talk to her about, and he was definitely interested in learning more about her and Olin's people among the clouds.

Mrs. Johnson came into the room. She plopped into the chair with a sigh. "I am so thankful tomorrow is Friday. Have you got plans for tomorrow, honey?"

Wil shrugged and muted the television. "We might go to Sally's. Have you heard back on that job?"

She shook her head. "Not yet, but you know how it goes, red tape and all. Hopefully, it will be some time next week." She grew silent and studied her son.

"What is it?" Wil asked when the silence lasted longer than a minute.

"Wil, honey, I need to talk to you about something, and I don't know... I don't know how you're going to take it."

Wil felt a cold stone settle in the pit of his stomach. He tried to make a joke out of it. "Mom, that's never a good way to start a conversation."

She smiled and leaned forward, her arms resting on her legs, her hands clasped in front of her.

"It's good news, actually. At least, I think it is."

He waited. "Well, if it's good news, why don't you tell me?" He hadn't seen his mother this nervous since the night she had to tell him that his dad was dying. The cold stone in his stomach grew a little.

"Okay." She took a deep breath. "You know your dad has been gone for almost three years now." The stone grew a little more. "And, well, nothing will ever change how much I loved him. I still do, but I can't... I can't live for a ghost. It's too hard."

Wil didn't say anything. His mouth felt dry. The TV flashed silent commercials at him. His mother stood up and began pacing.

"The thing is, honey, I've, well, I've met someone. He's a real nice guy, funny, sweet." She sat again. Wil refused to look at her.

"It's not serious," she rushed to explain. "I mean, I've only just met him, a few weeks ago. We've had coffee a couple of times, and he took me to dinner after my meeting the other night. I wanted to tell you about it beforehand, but then Scott showed up, and it just didn't seem to be the right time. I just wanted you to know." She paused. Her anxiety danced around the room. Wil didn't know what to say. He sat on the couch, feeling the cold spread from his stomach to his fingertips. When he finally managed to look at his mom, he saw hopefulness mixed with worry on her attractive face.

"He…he wants to take me out Saturday night, but I told him I couldn't go until I had talked to you first. Honey, please say something."

Wil spoke as though a robot; his voice sounded distant, as though from a dream. "That's great, Mom. You should go."

She slid over onto the sofa beside him. "Wil, I want you to be okay with this, so please tell me if you're not. I know this is coming as a shock, and I'm sorry. Please tell me how you feel."

"I'm fine," Wil replied mechanically. "I have to get ready for tomorrow. Good night." He got up and left the den, his mom still sitting on the couch. Climbing the steps to his room, Wil had the odd sensation of being detached from his body. Once in his room, he shut the door and lay down on his bed. The picture of his dad and him with their baseball gloves stared back at him. Wil heard his mother coming upstairs, the creak of the loose floorboards betraying her steps. He heard her bedroom door shut, and he hated himself.

CASSIA DID MAKE IT TO Wil's that night, but not before he had fallen into a fitful slumber. She lingered inside his window, her legs crossed in a sitting position, even though she hovered several feet off the ground. She gazed at him; he seemed surrounded by a heavy something Cassia could not identify and did not understand.

She noticed a picture clasped in his hand. Allowing herself to touch down gently on his floor, she moved over to him and took the picture from his hand, careful not to disturb him. Stepping back to the window, she held out her hand. A small orb of light began to grow. She held it up to the picture. A young boy with a strange brown leather hand stood beside an adult with a similar brown leather hand. Both looked happy. Cassia saw a striking similarity between the Wil she knew now and the adult in the picture: the same twinkling brown eyes and dimpled chins. The adult's hair flopped over his forehead like Wil's but was a deeper shade of brown. The adult had a pleasant face, handsome and gentle, with a slight edge to his nose.

After returning the picture to the nightstand, she focused on Wil. His face revealed only some of the internal struggle known only to him. Samson's words came back to her: "He may very well hold onto his innocence. You are to see that he does."

"What troubles you, Wil Johnson?" she whispered into the darkness. The orb floated just above her head. "What threatens your innocence?"

At that moment, she felt a sudden connection—instant, strong—with Wil, though she did not know from where it came. She studied him for a moment before making up her mind.

Kneeling by his bed, she placed her index and middle fingers and thumb across his forehead, her touch light so as not to wake him. Closing her eyes, she opened herself up to him. Images began to take shape in her mind, images of a young boy tossing an orange and black ball towards a hoop mounted on a pole outside, of a man lifting the boy so he could reach the hoop and successfully drop the ball through, of the man and boy sudsing up a four-wheeled vehicle with soap and spraying it with water. In the distance, Cassia saw herself, lingering just out of eye sight.

Cassia felt quiet bliss accompany the pictures. She didn't puzzle at the images; she knew she was an uninvited spy to Wil's subconscious, and such visions would make sense only to him. Slowly, though, the images began to change. Cassia saw the same man lying in a bed in a strange room. He appeared thin, wasted away, his rich thick hair now gray and nearly gone. The young boy sat in a chair near the bed, the baseball cap on his head. Nearby stood a woman with an attractive face and a second man with no face; this man held the woman in his arms. In the background, a faint image grew more and more visible, the shrieking louder and louder until the banshee was the only discernible image.

The contentment left Wil, and Cassia felt the heavy strangeness fall upon her again. She struggled against it, but it was just too intense. She couldn't shake it off and she couldn't detach herself from Wil; her power seemed to have vanished. It became more difficult for her to breathe. From somewhere in the distance, she heard a soft whimper.

A new struggle began to develop. The images were being forced down, not by Cassia but by Wil. She fought to maintain her connection. As the image of the frail man began to dissipate, a more majestic being galloped across Wil's subconscious. As the one-horned steed came into focus, Cassia felt the weighty unknown lift but not disappear. Hope drifted in alongside it, not completely balancing out, but making it easier for Cassia to maintain connection. The banshee screamed at the sight of the unicorn and spit hatred at the girl in white who stood nearby. Cassia saw herself beside the unicorn and felt the longing swell within Wil.

Sensing the coming dawn, she closed herself to Wil and lifted her hand from his forehead. The orb hovered nearby. She waved her hand, removing it from sight. Early morning sunrays peeked in through the open window.

Wil stirred awake, the strange heaviness still around him. He started in surprise to see Cassia sitting in the window, then threw his arm over his eyes.

"I looked for you last night," he said in a tired voice.

"I was here."

He looked at her. "When?"

"While you meditated." She smiled at him, and Wil felt better until she added, "I know of the images you saw, of the banshee and the unicorn."

Wil sat up and threw his legs over the side of the bed. He stared down at his feet. "She's real, isn't she?" He met her gaze. "The banshee's real?"

"Yes, she is very real."

"What does that mean? Is she part of Meslo's world?"

Cassia felt the room swell with that heavy something again. She channeled her energy on Wil.

"The banshee represents the lost innocence of humans. She exists in all humans. Born out of the same pit as Meslo's children, she exists to destroy the purity given by Olin to the people of this planet."

"So I keep seeing her because?" Wil shrugged his unspoken question at her. His eyes seemed dull in the morning light.

"Because she wants your innocence. As long as you believe, you maintain a virtue that is threatening to her. It is all a part of the Balance."

"Good versus evil." Wil sighed and stood. "So that's why you are here, to keep my soul from being taken over by a banshee. What am I supposed to do with that? It's too unreal to be anything but."

Cassia puzzled at the tone of his voice. "Wil, I am not here for your soul. That cannot be helped by anyone but you."

"Great." He paced the length of his bedroom. "I get a creature of fantastical powers to guide me through this life, only she can't guide me. And the balance of good and evil is shifting in my life, but that can't be helped, either, can it? So just why are you here?"

Cassia blinked as the wild and violent sensations assaulted her again. This time, however, she was able to steel herself against them.

"I am here for you, Wil Johnson."

"Yeah, that's what you keep saying. You're here for me, but

you're not here for me. You tell me stories, but meanwhile, some banshee is going to pop out in the middle of the night and what? Cart me off to Meslo in his underground lair? I'm not even supposed to be seeing you, but I do, and what is it getting me exactly?"

His frustration spilled over, and he turned his back on her. She saw him exhale and the droop of his shoulders. Walking over to him, she reached for one of his hands and held it in her own. Her calm blue eyes found his tortured brown ones; the tears that had threatened to spill over vanished as great serenity filled Wil. He stood perfectly still as bliss washed over him, beating down the confusion and frustration of last night. The smile from her mouth found its way to her eyes, and Wil honestly believed that everything would be all right.

"I am here for *you*, Wil. Do you understand?"

He nodded. "Yes. I'm sorry. It's just…a lot happened last night, and I don't know what to do with it. I don't know what to feel about it."

"You feel what you feel. You have to if you are to understand it." She squeezed his hand and let go, taking the sensations with her. Still, Wil didn't feel bad; rather, he felt a little stronger emotionally.

He glanced at his clock; it read 6:02 a.m.

"Do you think, um, you could tell me some more about the Balance?"

She smiled. "Yes. That is why I came, for what I have to tell you concerns you. Do you feel up to that?"

Wil's interest was piqued in spite of everything else. "Don't tell me—I really am going to be tempted by the banshee and the Balance will tip in favor of evil."

Cassia stared at him, but when he grinned, so did she. "Do you remember all I told you about the Great Battle?"

Wil nodded and sat in his computer chair. "Yeah. Olin gave humans the knowledge of magic, then took it away again." He shook his head and fidgeted with his baseball cap lying on the desk. "What a waste. Maybe the world would be a better place if we still had knowledge of that magic."

"What would you do with it, Wil?"

Wil looked at the picture of his dad hanging on the wall. "I'd keep people from suffering needlessly," he said almost to himself. "No one would die."

"Everyone dies, Wil. That is the nature of your people."

"Yeah, well, it shouldn't happen until people are really, really old." He slapped his baseball cap against his knee.

"Yes," she said after a moment. "I should think you would be a Restorer."

Their eyes met briefly. Wil stood and began pulling clothes out of his dresser. "In the days of Robin Hood, maybe."

Cassia sat on his bed. "Not quite. There were still a favored few who, even after the Great Battle had ended, were given Olin's blessings again. But their numbers have been very few."

"What, you mean there's some guy walking around out there right now, waving his hand over a broken leg, saying 'Heal thyself,' and it's working? I don't think so."

"No. That kind of magic was taken back to the realm from which it came. However, Olin recognized that some of Earth's children still possessed rationality, understanding, and the thirst for knowledge. To these, he bestowed another kind of blessing—the ability to *see* the magic." Cassia watched him closely. He stopped fussing with his shorts and turned towards her. She continued as he lowered himself into his chair.

"To these humans, Olin gave the knowledge of the Balance and the knowledge of the existence of magic. These people were a special brood; they had a deep belief in all things fantastical. Olin made them Secret Keepers, and they had the ability to see Olin's children and communicate with them."

Wil's eyes widened as he began to understand her words. "Then you mean..."

"Yes, Wil Johnson. You have that ability which makes you able to see me. You have the ability to be a Secret Keeper."

"A blessing of Olin?" he whispered. She smiled and nodded. "That's why no one else sees you the way you are. To them, you're just another girl, but you're not."

"No, I am not. And you are no longer just another boy. This ability you have carries with it great responsibilities. You will see things that no one else can. You must not expect to be able to discuss them with Scott or any of your other friends who do not possess a similar ability."

"What exactly am I supposed to do?" A nervous, excited fluttering filled his stomach where, only a few short hours ago, there had existed a cold emptiness.

"Only what you have already been doing: educating me in the ways of your people. Ours will be an exchange of information. You will come to understand my people as I come to understand yours. In this way, our two worlds will be united."

Wil took a deep breath. This seemed as a dream to him. "But what about the bad guys? What if Meslo returns? What happens then?"

The seriousness in her eyes stopped him from asking further questions.

"That is the one responsibility that carries the greatest consequence." She stood. "Should Meslo return, you can never reveal to him what you know of my world. It was the betrayal of our former Secret Keepers which enticed Olin into battle with Meslo. Those humans were seduced by the promise of power and control, and they proved disloyal to the one who had given them blessings of fortune and grace. It is not an easy task you undertake, but the responsibility is yours."

"What if I don't want it?" Wil stood up, suddenly too anxious to remain seated.

"Then you will be given a draught which will remove this

ability from you. I will disappear, and so will the knowledge you have already been given. You will remember nothing."

Wil stared at her. "You would leave?"

"I would not exist to you."

He thought only a moment more. "Fine. I accept this ability. I want it."

She smiled. "I thought you might."

Chapter 6

Wil slipped out of the house early. He didn't want to see his mom or to continue their talk from the night before. Besides, the idea of being a Secret Keeper weighed first and foremost on his mind. It was that thought that occupied his mind as he walked to the bus stop, where he met Scott coming up the sidewalk.

"Whoa, this is early," Scott commented, his voice tired and lacking its usual energy. "I was hoping for some breakfast. Old Mother Hubbard's cupboard is kinda empty, you know?"

"Yeah. Here." Wil passed his friend a pop-tart. He eyed the sandy blond boy carefully. "Something happened last night, didn't it?"

Scott chewed on his breakfast and shook his head. "Too much Nina Selna, you know?" He tapped the side of his head and continued eating.

Wil didn't believe him. His look said as much. Scott sighed.

"He just had a bad day yesterday, that's all. There was a lot of… yelling, and I didn't get much sleep last night. Honest."

"We can tell somebody; we can tell my mom," Wil said suddenly. "She'll know what to do about it."

"No way, man. Think about it, Wil. They'll haul my dad off to some cell to dry out for a few days, and I'll get put in some foster home. And what about our game today? No, I'll be okay."

"Scott—"

It's just a little lost sleep. No biggie. That's why God created math class." Scott took another bite of the pop-tart.

"Okay, fine," Wil consented after a moment. "But you're staying at my house tonight. Any time you want, really. Just come on over."

Friend considered friend for a moment.

"'Kay," Scott consented as the bus pulled alongside them. "Thanks."

Wil waved it aside and climbed onto the bus. He settled into the seat and stared out the window. He and Scott said nothing else on the ride to school. Outside the window drifted a thin wisp of cloud.

THE BASEBALL GAME WAS INTO the sixth inning. Wil glanced at the score board as he waited for his teammates to take their positions: Home-2, Visitor-2. He stretched out his arm and picked up the chalk rag at his feet. He tossed it in his left hand a couple of times. Scott trotted out to meet him on the mound.

"All right. Here's the deal. It's Trotman, Kelp, and Ayscue up first," Scott advised. "Trotman's having trouble hitting the curve today, so expect that to be the first call. Kelp's too fast on the swing, so you might want to use the change up. Ayscue gets the heater."

"I don't know if you noticed or not," Wil replied, "but Ayscue drove in the tying run two innings ago off my heater."

"True, but he didn't get to bat last inning, so he's going to be antsy for a swing, for one, and for two, his girlfriend just got here. He hasn't been able to tear himself away from the fence in the last four minutes. You just leave him to me."

"You're the boss," Wil consented. He glanced around the field. His mom sat in the stands with the other parents. Scott's dad wasn't there. Down the right field line, past first base, Wil noticed a certain shaggy-haired boy leaning against the fence.

"Did you see Andrew down there?" he asked Scott as the umpire dusted off home plate.

"Yeah. He's been there since the third inning. Don't worry about him. Remember, curve, slow, heater." Scott and Wil slapped their gloves together, and Scott trotted back to home plate as the first batter stepped up to the plate.

Wil waited for the signal from Scott. He nodded once to show he understood, then pulled the ball into his glove. Going into a wind up, he let the ball loose. It spiraled at chest level right to the outer edge of the plate before curving downward into Scott's glove.

"Strike!" called the umpire.

Scott returned the ball and settled back in a squat position. Wil waited, nodded, wound up, and threw. The same pitch, the same results, only this time the batter swung and missed.

"Strike two!"

Scott nodded to himself and returned the ball. The first base coach called to the batter, gave a few signals, then clapped encouragement.

The batter stepped back to the plate and steadied the bat at chest level. Wil went into his wind up and threw.

"Strike three!" cried the umpire as the batter swung and missed a second time.

"All right, all right!" Scott called out, throwing the ball to Derek at first base, who promptly tossed it to the second baseman. "One down! One down!"

Wil waited for the ball to return to him. He again noticed Andrew against the fence. His nemesis watched with great interest; his eyes followed the ball around the field. Wil noticed this time that Andrew had a book in his hands, a book that he was making notations in as he watched the field.

The ball found its way back to Wil's glove. He waited for Kelp to get set at the plate, then watched for Scott's signal. Going into the wind up, he released the ball. As Scott had said, Kelp was fast on the swing, and the ball crossed home plate after his follow-thru.

Wil heard his mom cheering. He ignored her and got set for the second pitch. Out of the corner of his eye, he noticed Andrew writing in the book. He wound up and threw another slow pitch ball. This time, however, Kelp waited and foul tipped it straight up. Scott threw off his mask and looked up. The ball fell into this glove.

Wil's mom cheered again as Scott tossed the ball around the field again.

"That's two!" he called out, holding up his first and fourth fingers.

The third batter got set as Wil caught the ball and kicked dirt out of his mound. He watched Scott give the signal and set the ball in his hand.

"Hey, Ayscue," Scott said conversationally, "saw your girl-friend over there."

Wil went into his wind up.

"She's pretty hot. Tell me, you think she'd be interested in hit-ting a nudist's beach sometime?"

The fast ball sailed across the plate, and Ayscue swung on nothing but air. The ball plopped into Scott's glove. He grinned to himself and tossed it back to Wil. Settling back, he gave Wil the signal.

"'Course," Scott continued unabashedly as Wil went into his wind up. "It's not likely she can top your sister … topless."

Again, the ball sailed over the plate. Ayscue waited a second too late to swing and again caught air. He gave Scott a dirty look and reset himself.

Wil got his signal and took the ball into his glove.

"Hey, no hard feelings," Scott spoke genially. "Maybe we can all get together sometime …"

Wil went into his wind up.

"Your sister, your girlfriend, your mom, and me. What's that called? An orgy?"

Crack! The ball sailed up high and plummeted down in a "V" shape, right into Derek's waiting glove.

Scott cackled to himself as Ayscue glared at him.

"That's three," Scott informed him before trotting to his team's dugout.

"I don't know what you said to him," Derek commented as the boys settled on the bench, "but he looks mad as hell."

"I'm telling you, man, a girlfriend at a ballgame is just asking for trouble."

"Yeah, like *you'll* ever find out," Taylor, the centerfielder, ragged.

"Hey, I'm working my groove," Scott informed them.

"Cushman, Jenkins, Seater, you guys are up!" the coach called out.

"All right, Davey!" Derek cheered as the batter stepped up to the plate. "It's all you, man!"

Wil drank a cup of water and put his team jacket on. He watched as Davey took two balls and a strike before cranking it down the third base line. He just missed making it to first base.

"That's all right! Good try, Davey," Wil cheered as his teammate trotted back into the dugout. Right above left field floated a thin, wispy cloud. Wil leaned out of the dugout and stared at it. A smile tugged at the corners of his mouth. He joined in his team cheering for Scott as his friend took his stance at the plate.

The first pitch was low and outside.

Wil watched the cloud drift towards right field. The second pitch was high and inside, a little too inside. Scott tilted back just as it sailed over the plate. Wil's team jeered and booed.

"Oh, man, I hope he gets this one. We need this hit," Derek worried next to Wil. He leaned on the fence to watch.

"He will. He's due." Wil watched as Scott steadied the bat level and pulled it back on his shoulder. When the next pitch came, *CRACK!* Bat met ball over the plate.

Wil and his teammates pressed against the fence, following the ball with their eyes. It sailed towards right field, dropping down in between the center and right fielders. Wil's team cheered as Scott round first and slid into second safely.

"Seater, you're up!" the assistant coach called out. "Cooper, on deck. Bryson, you're next!"

Wil watched as Scott took his lead from second base. He marveled at his friend's concentration; regardless of what his home life was like, when it came to baseball, Scott had a one-track mind.

Seater cranked one out to right field; Scott waited until the right fielder caught it, then tagged up. Wil heard his mother cheering loudly. He chuckled to himself and shook his head.

"Come on, Derek! Bring him home!" Wil coached from the dugout.

Derek took two balls and a strike. Scott led off third but dove back when the pitcher tried to pick him off. On the next pitch, Derek drove the ball over the shortstop's head. Scott raced home while Derek sprinted to first. The score stood three to two now. Wil high-fived Scott in the dugout.

"Nice hit," he complimented.

"Thanks. Your mom is a trip. She's got to be the loudest one out there." Scott shook his head, but the grin belied his pleasure. He attached the shin guards to his legs and reached for the chest pad.

"Yeah." Wil stared at his shoes for a moment. He couldn't help feeling a little resentful. For her to start seeing someone else . . . at the same time, she had been to most of his games. He couldn't deny that he would have missed her being here today. "It's like having our own personal cheerleader without the pom-poms."

"Or the short skirt."

Wil punched him in the arm. Scott shrugged as Bryson struck out.

"Hey, you brought it up."

The two of them followed their team out to the field.

"All right, all right, seventh inning!" Scott called out, his catcher's mask and mitt in his hands. "All we need is three, fellas!"

He joined Wil on the mound and surveyed the line-up for the other team. Derek and Davey Cushman, the third baseman, joined them.

"All right, their three best hitters are coming up," Derek said.

"One of them's a lefty," Scott added. "Your curve's been dropping to the left side of the plate, so you may be able to get him on the inside corner."

"Yeah, and they're down one," Davey chimed in, "so we've got to expect them to go for the hits. We'll play deep."

Wil rotated his left shoulder. "That Lauder kid's been beating us up on the left side."

"You just get it over the plate," Scott counseled. "We'll take care of the rest."

The four boys slapped gloves and separated. Wil threw a few warm-ups while waiting for the umpire to start the inning. He noticed Derek and Davey passing the word around. His infield backed up to the edge of the dirt; the outfielders pushed back towards the fence.

The umpire called the first batter to the plate. Wil bent over the mound and waited for Scott's signal. He shook off the first signal but liked the second one. Scott set himself, and Wil went into his wind-up. The ball left his hand and sailed towards home plate. At the last second, it dropped wide.

Scott threw it back to him and reset. Wil shook off the first signal but took the second one again. Winding up, he let loose another curve ball; this one still fell wide, but the batter swung. The ball sailed down the third base line, foul.

On the third pitch, the batter cracked one wide to left field. Wil watched it sail in a low arc; John Seater charged after it, catching it just before it hit the ground.

He exhaled. "Nice job, Seater!"

"That's one!" Scott called from the plate, his finger in the air.

The second batter up was the lefty. Wil stretched out his arm; over his team's dugout hung the wispy cloud. He ignored the flush of excitement he felt when he thought of seeing her again. There was much more he wanted to hear about her people, but right now, he needed to keep his head in this game.

He bounced the chalk rag off his hand and leaned forward to wait for Scott's signal. He took the first one and pitched.

The curve ball dropped on the inside corner.

"Strike one!" called the umpire. Scott nodded in approval and threw the ball back.

On the second pitch, the batter foul tipped it behind the umpire. Scott scampered for it, but missed it by inches. He threw it back to Wil and grinned at something the umpire said to him. After resetting, he gave Wil the signal. The ball sailed towards the plate, and flew off the end of the bat. It dropped in the gap in centerfield, but the batter held up at first.

When Lauder came up, he took the first pitch and knocked it clean to the left. John Seater was too far to the right to get it, Dylan Snyder was too far to the left of it. Wil watched in dismay as Lauder reached second base. He glanced at the runner on third before catching the ball in his glove. Scott called time-out and trotted out to the mound.

"Hey, forget it," he said without waiting. "You can do this. What have you got to give me?"

"I don't know," Wil answered honestly. "My arm feels like jelly." He glanced again at the runner on third.

"Hey, forget about them. You just get that ball across the plate; that's your job. Stay with me, buddy. I don't want to finish with Rorco." Scott tapped him in the shoulder with his mitt.

Wil nodded, and Scott headed back to home plate, calling out "One out!" again. Wil took a deep breath and shook out his arm. He saw Mike Rorco warming up in the make-shift bull pen.

The next batter up was little on the heavy side. Wil could almost see the inner cogs turning in Scott's mind.

"Come on, buddy, help me out," he said to himself, leaning over to wait for the signals. He shook off the first two signals

Scott gave him. On the third signal, he nodded and went into his wind-up.

"Say, did you see the warning they put out about Hostess cupcakes?" Scott asked as he waited for the pitch. Wil released the ball. "They've been recalled for salmonella."

The batter swung and missed.

"Strike one!"

"'Course, I guess that's better than hot dogs. You know, my cousin," (Wil took the signal and went into his wind-up) "found an actual rat's tail sticking out the end of hers. Nasty."

The batter hesitated, casting an amazed glance at Scott. The ball fell right into his glove.

"Strike two!"

Scott refused to meet his eyes. He threw the ball back and sat on the balls of his feet.

"I don't know, man. It's like nothing's safe to eat anymore. Salmonella, rat's tails, a dog's toenail, which my girlfriend actually found in one of those fast food hamburgers. 'Course, she had already taken a bite, so it was in her *mouth* before she realized it was there—" The ball popped up to Rodney Toll at second base. He caught it easily.

Scott looked at the batter then, his mask pushed up to reveal the grin on his face. "I hear you guys are stopping at Sally's on the way out. I'd get the chicken sandwich if I was you."

The batter returned to the dugout, looking a little green around the gills.

"That's two!" Scott announced, holding up his fingers. Wil grinned at him and shook his head. Whatever he was in the classroom, Scott was definitely a force to be reckoned with on the ball field.

Settling back on the mound for the next batter, Wil noticed that Andrew had edged closer towards first base. He watched the game intently, and right now he was paying a good deal of attention to Wil.

Wil caught the ball and flipped it in his hand in an effort to ignore his nemesis. He wiped the sweat off his forehead, then leaned forward. Scott made the call, and Wil threw a sinker. The batter laid off of the pitch, which was a strike.

Wil waited for the next signal; he noticed Andrew was parallel with first base now. He seemed to be staring at the ball in Wil's hand, curiosity written all over his face.

Ignoring him, Wil shook off each of Scott's signals. His arm was tired; he wasn't sure he could make anything else. Scott went through the signals again, and Wil nodded on the last one, the sinker. He threw, and the batter smacked it down the right field line. It went foul just before it hit first base.

"That's two!" Scott called out. "Two outs, two strikes! Here we go!"

"Come on, Wil," Derek encouraged. "You can do this!"

His teammates called out more encouragement, and Wil shook his arm loose again. Getting his signal, he pitched. The batter drove a grounder between Derek and Rodney; Derek dove for it and tossed it to Wil, who reached first base two steps ahead of the batter.

"Yes!" Scott cheered as Wil and Derek slapped gloves together. "Victory is ours!"

Wil lay wide awake, watching the morning sun creep over the horizon. Scott slept in the next room, worn out by the constant rehashing of each play of the game. Though he was tired, sleepiness eluded Wil; he stared out the open window, waiting, hoping. He was rewarded, for at that moment, she drifted into his room, her form solidifying at the foot of his bed.

"Greetings, Wil," she smiled at him. "Are you preparing to meditate? Should I ..." she sought for the correct words. "Come back at another time?"

"No." Wil kicked the covers off and stood up. "I've been

waiting for you. I saw you, well, your cloud at the game yesterday."

"Oh, yes. I enjoyed that very much, although I am not certain I understood what was happening. What do you call this ... game?"

He smiled. "It's called baseball. I don't guess you play anything like that up there."

She shook her head, then asked eagerly, "Could you explain it to me? The Council is very interested in these types of human activities. Why do you play it?"

"Well, because it's fun. See," he reached over to his desk and picked up his glove. His practice ball lay inside it. "The object is to score runs by hitting this ball. If you hit this ball, you run the bases, those, um, lumps in the ground. You want to run around all three bases and come back to where you started, home plate. If you do that, your team gets a run, a point scored."

"And you use those sticks to hit the ball. What are they called?"

"Bats. And this is a glove." He held it out to her. She took it and examined it thoroughly. "You use this to catch the ball so you don't hurt your hand."

"You kept running on and off the field," she said, still examining the glove. "Sometimes you used the bat, and sometimes you used the glove." She passed it back to him. "How do you know when you are supposed to be using which?"

"Well, one team gets to hit with the bat. The team with the gloves has to try to get three outs. If the team with the gloves gets three outs, then they get to use the bats."

"And you get three outs by catching the ball in the glove?"

"That's one way. Another way, we can throw it to each other to tag out a runner, or we can strike them out, throw balls they can't hit. If they get three of those, it's an out."

"Is this something that all young humans know to do, this baseball?"

Wil shrugged. "I guess. I mean, my dad taught me when I was little. He taught Scott, too. He wanted me to play short stop, where he played, but I like pitching too much. That's what it's called when you try to throw balls they can't hit."

Cassia felt the fondness wash over him as he mentioned his dad. There was also something else, though, something heavy and oppressive.

"I have not seen your dad," she observed, watching him carefully. "Is he not around?"

Wil stared at his glove and ball and deliberately set them back on the computer desk. "No. No, he's not." He shook off the grief and turned towards her. "So? What, will you explain to the Council about baseball now?"

She studied him; there suddenly existed a cap on his emotions, some barrier she couldn't penetrate. She would have to remember to ask Samson about it.

"Yes, when I am called." The silence grew between them until she took his hands. Bliss washed over him, and he forgot the awkwardness. "I would like to show you something. Will you come?"

"Yeah."

She led him over to the window and smiled at him. "We must go up there." She faded suddenly into the mist and sailed through the window. Wi leaned his head out and saw her standing on the roof. Shaking his head in disbelief, he climbed out the window and pulled himself up on the gutter. With a light leap, he hoisted himself onto the slanted rooftop. He crawled up to sit beside her.

"Wow," he commented. The sunrise sprayed blue and orange across the sky in thick lines. The clouds drifting above were of various shapes and sizes; the morning light cast gray shadows around them.

"I wanted to tell you a little more about the clouds," she began, eyeing the sky.

Wil looked at her, his eyes bright and eager. She met his gaze, and he felt trapped in the two pools that were her eyes.

"I do not know if you have ever considered the various shapes above you, but they are indicative of what we do individually. For example," she pointed skyward, "those small, thin clouds there that look like me, those are the Gatherers. Our task is to communicate with our Secret Keepers and exchange information about this world," she looked at him, "and ours."

"And then you report it to the Council."

"Yes. Once we pass on our information to them, they make sure the rest of my people are aware, so that there is nothing that happens on the other side of this world that I do not know about. I may not understand fully, but I am aware of it."

"How do they do that? It's not like the sky is this big." Wil held up his hands a few inches apart and eyed her, amazed.

She thought about it before answering. "Our ... essences are interconnected. We are able to read each other, much like I can read you."

Wil felt some of the blood drain from his face. "You can *read* me?"

"Yes. I do not always understand the sensations, but I am aware of them. It is part of the relationship we have with our Secret Keepers. It was born out of necessity during the Great Battle.

"You see, when Meslo unleashed his children upon this world, they sought out the Secret Keepers first. They were able to manipulate and control those early Secret Keepers by turning their emotions against them. Once he realized this was happening, Olin bestowed upon us the ability to ... read the essences of our Secret Keepers. That way, should they be tempted by Meslo's children, we would be better able to help them fight the temptations. In that way, we became their Guardians as well."

Wil felt uneasy with this news. It wasn't as if he had anything to hide, but to know that his feelings weren't private unsettled him. She sensed as much and took his hand. Again, that feeling of bliss washed over him, and he felt calmer.

"Do not worry, Wil. It is not as if I am aware of your thoughts, per se. It is more of an emotional connection, which is why I do not always understand you."

He breathed a little easier and looked down at her hand held in his. "Is that why I can, um, *feel* you when you touch me?"

She smiled. "Yes. Does it trouble you?"

"No. No, not at all." The last thing he wanted was for her to remove her hand; it felt too good feeling good. "What are those clouds indicative of?" He pointed at fat clouds in the distance, clouds who, in their fatness, almost made lumpy circles.

"They are the Sentinels."

Wil puzzled. "Fighters? But I thought Olin was all about peace?"

She smiled, amused. "He is, but we had to have someone to battle Meslo and his children in the Great Battle. Olin specially trained certain of my people for this task. Once the Great Battle ended, those Sentinels began training others, so that should Meslo try to re-establish his army, we will be ready."

"But what do they do in the meantime? I mean, how long ago was the Great Battle? Do they spend *all* their time training?"

"No. Do not be fooled, Wil. Meslo has not been meditating all these many moons. His forces are on this earth at the rising of every sun. His…handprints are everywhere. Our Sentinels work constantly to either minimize his destruction or to prevent it from happening all together. I believe sometimes humans are witnesses to these struggles, although they do not realize what they are seeing."

"How's that?"

She pondered, searching for the best way to explain what she meant. "Have you ever heard rumbling from the sky?"

"Sure. During thunderstorms." Wil stared at her twinkling blue eyes. "You mean that's actually the Sentinels battling Meslo?"

"Yes. And the great flashes of light that can be seen—"

"Are actually one magic against another," Wil finished as understanding washed over him. "What's the sign if the cloud people win, rain?"

Her eyes drew together in puzzlement. "What do you mean?"

"Well, if thunder and lightning represent the actual battle, then there has to be some kind of sign proving who the winner is."

"No one side ever wins, Wil. No one side *can* win."

"Because of the Balance."

"Yes."

"So what does the rain have to do with the battles?"

"The Lethean Rains are a cleanser; any knowledge a human has of the battles is unremembered after the rains come. It does not affect Secret Keepers, however."

She grew quiet, thoughtful, and Wil felt something pull at the serenity he felt. It was too deep and too complex for him to understand, but it was there. After a moment, she pulled her hand away, and all the sensations vanished.

"What is it?" he asked, suddenly concerned.

"Nothing." She looked at him, and her blue eyes looked a little darker. "Nothing for you to be concerned with." She turned her gaze back to the sky, and continued their conversation as if they had not been interrupted. "You can tell the experience of our Sentinels by the size of the cloud. That one there," she pointed to her right, and Wil reluctantly followed her finger up. The cloud she pointed to was huge; its roundness was broken by several puffs trailing off it like petals off a flower.

"That is Devlin. He fought in the Great Battle, but he is also part of the Council. See the volume of his shape? That is because he is one of the most experienced Sentinels we have. He was one of the first that Olin trained, and his courage is second only to Olin's.

"Now see that one over there?" She shifted and pointed to a much smaller cloud drifting lazily southward. "That is Astin. He is young, like me. He was not created until after the Great Battle was many moons past, and his experience is not as vast."

"Soooo," Wil drawled, "you're inexperienced in your area? Gathering?"

She smiled at him, and the morning sun glowing on them heightened the glory of that smile. "You are my first."

Wil flushed lightly. "Well, you're pretty good at it," he mumbled.

"It is for what I was created."

Just then, Scott's head popped out of the window beneath them.

"What the hell are you doing?" he asked, amused.

Wil glanced at Cassia. She shook her head silently at him. "Watching the sun rise."

"By yourself? That's kind of a waste." Scott scrambled onto the roof and plopped down beside Wil. "Wow. Look at that. You can see the whole neighborhood."

"I know. Pretty neat, huh?"

"Oh, hey, your mom's making French toast. And sausage! I could smell it all the way upstairs."

"She usually does on Saturdays."

Scott tucked his knees up to his chest and wrapped his arms around them. He rocked back and forth gently. "I guess I'd better eat and get home before my old man realizes I'm gone. He's probably starting to sober up by now."

"Scott," Wil sighed. "You should just stay here. My mom won't care."

"It'll be fine." Scott waved off his concern. "He'll be in the garage most of the day, tinkering with that stupid car. You know, the one that doesn't work because he wrecked it six years ago?"

"I still think you ought to tell somebody. My mom will know what to do."

"I told you no." Scott looked annoyed. "I ain't going to a group home or into foster care. Do you know that if they send me to a foster family, it could be miles from here? And that group home has a curfew. I wouldn't be able to pop over and hang out. No, huh-uh. And you gotta swear you won't tell anybody, either."

"Have I ever?" Wil demanded.

"Well, I don't know. You're getting all motherly on me."

"That's because it's getting *worse*, Scott. You know it, and I know it."

Scott shook his head stubbornly. "All I have to do is hang in there for a few more years. Once we graduate, I'm outta there, and this year is almost over with. You know I'll be over here most of the summer, so that'll be okay. Just promise me you won't say anything."

Wil shook his head to show is disapproval. "Okay. I won't say anything."

"Thanks." Scott stared off in the distance for a moment. "Hey, look, breakfast is probably ready. You coming?"

"Yeah. I'm right behind you."

Scott scooted to the edge of the roof, rolled over on his stomach, and dropped halfway over the edge. Finding his footing, he lowered himself the rest of the way and disappeared into the bedroom.

Wil sighed and glanced at Cassia. Her expression was hard to read.

"You are concerned for him."

"Yeah." Wil looked at the sky for a moment. "But I guess he knows what he's doing."

"And if he does not?"

Wil stared at her; he didn't have an answer. She smiled then, taking some of the gloom away.

"You have a good heart, Wil. Remember that." She stood up. "Now I must go. It is time. It is time for you as well."

He looked up at her, squinting in the bright morning sun. "See you later?"

She nodded and floated away, her cloud form taking over as she went. Wil followed her with his eyes until she was swallowed up by the bright blue above. Then he scooted to the edge of the roof and climbed down.

At the breakfast table, Scott busily chewed his way through

the plate of toast and sausage. Nora watched him, her gentle brown eyes studying his face. She looked up when Wil came in.

"Good morning, honey. There's toast in the oven for you."

"Thanks, mom." Wil busied himself with his breakfast.

"So what do you two have planned for today?" she asked conversationally.

"Oh, I've got to get home," Scott replied. "I promised my dad I would be home early. He wants us to see if we can get the transmission fixed on that car."

Wil sat down at the table, careful to keep his eyes averted. He marveled at how well Scott told the lie. It frightened him a little.

Nora kept her eyes on him as she sipped her coffee. "How's he doing?" she asked carefully. "With his ... problem? Is he still going to AA?"

Scott nodded emphatically. "Twice a week. He's making really good progress, too. Well, there was a little set back last week; he had to call his sponsor, but they got it worked out."

"Uh-huh." Nora's eyes flickered from Scott to her son. Wil had to remind himself not to gawk at his friend. He worked to keep his face neutral by taking a large forkful of French toast. Nora's gaze settled back on Scott.

"And how are you doing, Scott? You look tired."

Scott hesitated eating; Wil could almost hear the cogs of his mind turning, formulating some lie.

"I'm good," he answered after a moment. "I've just been trying to keep my grades up. It's not as easy for some of us as it is for others."

Wil shot him a look over the rim of his orange juice glass. Scott kept his eyes on his plate, doing his best to remain upbeat.

Nora set down her coffee cup. "Maybe I'll stop by some time, say hello."

Wil saw the first crack appear in Scott's façade. He chewed slowly on a piece of sausage, hesitating.

"That'd be good. He'd like that." Wil didn't think Scott sounded nearly as convincing as he hoped. He gulped down the last of his orange juice and stood. "Well, I gotta get going. Thanks, Mrs. J., for letting me crash and for breakfast." He set the dirty dishes in the kitchen by the sink. "I'll see you, Wil."

As he started out of the kitchen, Nora stood and hugged him close to her. Wil stared in surprise; Scott looked startled by the action. However, when she released him, he forced a smile.

"Breakfast *and* a hug. Bet you can't get that at any hotel."

"You call us if you need anything," Nora said seriously.

Scott nodded. "We will. Bye, Wil." He turned and hurried from the house.

Nora turned back to her son. "Is he? Okay, I mean?"

Wil swallowed and shrugged. "He says he is."

Nora studied him for a moment. Wil wasn't sure what she was looking for, and he wasn't sure whether she found it or not. After a moment, she reached for her coffee cup and refilled it.

"I've got to get started on the bills for this month. Do you mind cleaning up the kitchen?"

"Not a problem." Wil felt a sudden rush of relief now that the conversation seemed over. He finished eating, thankful for the quiet that had settled over the house, then stood and began loading the dishwasher.

"BASEBALL." CHARLIE LET THE WORD play on his lips while he reached through the recesses of time. "Yes, we are familiar with it, although it has only ever been perceived through the eyes of a human adult."

Cassia stood before the Council, having just given her report. She noticed Jereni seemed preoccupied with some thought; her eyes focused unseeingly on some task far away.

"The views of the younger humans shed a much different perspective on the play," Devlin remarked. "Your Wil Johnson, for example, is deeply connected to this activity. Any idea why?"

"I believe it has something to do with his father guardian. He said he was taught to play by what he called his 'dad.' There is also the attachment it gave him to the one called 'Scott.' Wil is … connected to him more so than anyone else his age."

She noticed Jereni's eyes flickered to her when she mentioned Scott's name. The reason eluded her, however; the elders had much more control in keeping their essences closed off from the youngsters.

"Thank you, Cassia. We will continue to explore this new perspective you have brought to us." Rebecca smiled at her, and the Council members stood. Cassia followed Samson out of the great hall.

"Samson, can I ask you about something?"

"Of course, Cassia." He stopped and waited for her to catch up. "It was wise of you to explain the bonding to your Wil Johnson. It is important that he understands how deeply he is bound to you."

"It is about that I wish to discuss with you." Cassia paused. "I do sense many emotions from him, and you were right; I do not understand all of them. However, something happened when he mentioned his father guardian. I … lost my focus with him during that conversation. It was as if some great wall separated our essences from one another."

Samson nodded thoughtfully. "You are not the first to experience this, Cassia. All Gatherers encounter this separation at one time or another with their Secret Keepers. I have been studying this for many moons, and I think I am just beginning to understand why that separation occurs.

"You see, all humans experience hardships at one time or another in their lives. With these hardships come periods of clarity and then periods of confusion. They do not often know how to accept what has happened to them or maybe they accept it but feel unable to move forward with their lives.

"Being that you are bound to Wil Johnson now, one of two things may be occurring. If he is unable to accept whatever hardship has befallen him concerning his father guardian, then there will be a blank spot on his essence, void of emotions until he does accept the hardship. Of course, it could also be that humans have the ability to manipulate their emotions. If he is unwilling to feel the true emotion the hardship provokes, he may be manufacturing false emotions to keep the true feeling from surfacing. That would also cause a disconnect between your essences."

"Is this anything about which to be concerned?"

"Not immediately. But as his Guardian, you are bound to help him reconcile his emotions to strengthen his essence. Otherwise, he becomes a very easy target for Meslo's influence."

"Thank you, Samson. I will consider your words."

Samson nodded and started away. "Oh, and Cassia? Be prepared. Humans often are not able to deal with one hardship before another presents itself. The longer it takes your Wil Johnson to reconcile himself to his feelings, the more susceptible he becomes."

He nodded at her pointedly before being swallowed up by the cloud he was standing on. Cassia stared at the spot where he had been, considering his words. Then she allowed the same cloud to swallow her so she could meditate and hopefully find the answer to her problem.

Chapter 7

Wil hung up the phone. "Mom! Is it okay if I go to the movies with Scott and Chris?"

Nora came down the stairs, fastening an earring. "Of course, honey. Here you go." She went into her hand bag and pulled out a twenty dollar bill.

Wil stared at her, the cold stone resettling in his stomach. "You're awfully dressed up for Saturday night."

Although she wore jeans and a short-sleeved shirt, her hair was curled and tied with a scarf. She wore make-up and one of her best jewelry sets: earrings, necklace, bracelet.

She fidgeted, suddenly nervous. "Well, honey, remember I told you? I'm ... going out with Larry."

"From work?" Wil couldn't help but play dumb. The stone in his belly grew a little larger.

She took his hands in hers. "No, Wil. He's the guy I met, the one I've had coffee with a few times? It's real casual. We're just going to the community college. They're having a comedy show there tonight." She shrugged apologetically.

Wil nodded numbly and pulled his hands away from hers. "Fine. It's fine. Go. Have a good time."

"Wil, we need to talk about this. I want to know how you feel. I want you to be okay with this."

"I am. Can't you tell?" He glared at her for a moment, then

reached for his jacket. "I gotta go, or I'm gonna be late. Have fun on your *date*."

He stalked past her and slammed the door behind him. Walking away from the house didn't seem fast enough, so he started jogging, then broke into a sprint. He rounded the corner of the block before he slowed down. A car horn tooted at him, and Chris's head stuck out of the back seat window.

"Hey, Wil! We were on our way to your house. Come on, get in."

Wil climbed into the car without a word. He was too busy concentrating on thawing out the stone of ice that seemed stuck in his craw.

"Hey," Chris greeted him, "I heard you guys won the game last night. I would've been there, but *some*body got whiny about being out in the sun, so I couldn't go." The last few words were directed towards the younger girl in the front seat. She turned and stuck her tongue out at him. He made a face at her.

"Yeah," Scott replied from the other side of Chris. "Wil's building up a pretty good sinker, and his curve ball isn't bad, either. If I keep working with him, he might make a fairly decent pitcher one day."

Wil grinned, even though he didn't feel like it. "What are we going to see, anyway?"

"Oh, man! It's gonna be so great!" Scott enthused. "It's the new Johnny-O movie..."

Chris punched Scott in the leg and looked pointedly at the lady driving the car. She glanced in the rearview mirror at the three boys in the backseat.

Scott played it off. "You know, Wil, the, um, one about the group of high school students who, um, start a fundraiser to, uh, help ... free ... the dolphins from the tuna nets."

Chris stared at him in horror. Scott shrugged and shook his head. In spite of himself, Wil felt a chuckle rising in his throat and looked out the window so Chris's mom wouldn't see his grin.

"Yeah, yeah," Chris chimed in with false enthusiasm. "That's the one. Good quality family film."

Wil bit down on his lips to contain his sudden urge to laugh.

"Yep," Scott continued. "No violence whatsoever. None. Unless you count the canning of the tuna."

Wil snickered then and resolved himself to the silent giggles shaking his body. Chris scrunched down in the middle of the seat, his own mouth repressed against his laughter. Scott feigned innocent confusion over their humor, but when he turned towards his own window, a mischievous grin tugged at the corners of his mouth.

Chris's mom pulled up in front of the movie theater, and the three boys tumbled out.

"Thanks, mom. See you about ten-thirty." Chris stepped up onto the curb where Wil and Scott were giving in to their gales of laughter. He punched Scott in the arm as his mom drove away.

"I'm sorry," Scott said with fake remorse. "It was the best I could do on such short notice."

"Man!" Chris sighed. "If you would've kept talking, we'd be baby-sitting Gina at the 'good quality family film' instead of going to see some butt-kicking!"

The thought of seeing violence suddenly made Wil feel much better. At least he wouldn't have to pretend to be in a good mood. He followed the other two inside and bought his ticket.

When Wil got home later that evening, he went straight to his room. His mom wasn't home just yet, but he didn't want to be up when she did get home. He didn't want to continue their discussion, and he certainly didn't want to hear about her good time.

He kicked off his shoes and lay down on his bed. Staring out the open window, he was convinced sleep would elude him. He was wrong; before half-an-hour had passed, he had fallen into a deep, troubling sleep.

———————

THE NEXT DAY, HE SUCCEEDED in avoiding his mom. He stayed in his room most of the day on the pretense of doing his schoolwork; whenever he got hungry, he went downstairs and made a sandwich or stole a Klondike bar from the freezer. He didn't speak to his mom unless she spoke to him, but she seemed willing to give him some space. She even left a plate of food in the oven for him at dinner. Wil almost felt bad for the silence, but he couldn't bring himself to talk to her about it. What could she say that would make this betrayal okay?

He couldn't think of anything, so it was better to keep quiet. Besides, he kept hoping Cassia would show up, and he didn't want to be in a foul mood if she did. She didn't, and Sunday dragged on slowly.

The first of the week brought with it the pleasure of the escape to school. Wil felt comfortable in the routine; he didn't even mind the dreaded science. He took solace in the presence of his friends and, of course, Cassia. She showed up faithfully every day, masquerading as a student. As usual, she showed interest in everything around her, her curiosity never seeming satisfied.

However, Wil also noticed that some distraction hovered over her. On more than one occasion, he had caught her studying Scott, then himself. There seemed to be some puzzle between them she couldn't solve.

And then there was her continued interest in Andrew. Wil saw her try again to engage him in conversation and again, he blew her off, stalking past Wil with a fierce scowl, as if Wil had somehow put her up to it.

But life at home was unsettled, and the tension refused to let up. Wil didn't sleep at all, or if he did, he had troubling dreams involving faceless men dipping his mother on the dance floor while his dad, shriveled and wrinkled from the chemotherapy treatments, watched from the sidelines. One night, he dreamed that his dad, bound to a wheelchair, was being steadily lowered into a hole in the ground that reached much deeper than six feet. His mom stood by the hole, waving goodbye. Some faceless man held Wil by the arms several feet from the hole; Wil struggled in his arms, trying to get to the hole to save his dad, but it was to no avail.

Suddenly, from the hole, a giant hand made entirely of fire flames reached high into the air. Wil saw his dad in the palm of the hand, burning, screaming silent screams. His mom stepped away from the hole, smiling as the flaming hand disappeared underground again, taking his dad with him. The faceless man let go of Wil's arms to embrace his mom; Wil ran to the spot where the hole had been, only now there was a charred spot in the earth. His mom pulled him away and turned him to face the faceless man, who spoke though he had no mouth: *Hi, Wil, you can call me 'Dad.'*

Wil bolted upright from his sleep, his face drenched in sweat. He stared at the darkness of his bedroom, through which trickled only a sliver of light from the moon hanging above trees. Realizing it had only been a dream helped to slow his heartbeat. He swung his legs over the bed and held his head in his hands.

Because she chose to keep herself invisible to him, he couldn't see Cassia hovering just outside his window, her face puzzling over the sensations she sensed from him. She watched as he stood and moved to kneel beside the window. He stared up at the sky while trying to shake off the nightmare.

She studied his face, which was just inches from her; she could have touched it with her human hand if she had wanted. The dark something hung around him; she longed to give a name to it, but her limited experience kept her from recognizing his misery.

Below her, something green scuttled across the yard. It threw its pale green head back, wild hair sticking out in all directions, red lips glistening in the pale moonlight. When it cackled, two fangs showed.

Cassia watched the banshee silently. The creature scuttled back and forth, not able to get any closer than the tree in the front yard, shrieking one word into the night: "Mine!"

Wil stared sadly at nothing. He couldn't see the banshee; Cassia watched his face carefully for any sign that he had. There was none.

Cassia turned her attention back towards the creature.

"Mine! Mine!" it shrieked, still not able to get any closer than the tree.

Cassia produced an orb and held it in her hand for one moment. Then she flung it down, hitting the creature. The banshee *poofed!* out of existence.

Cassia stared at the spot the banshee had been. Her serious eyes slowly turned back towards Wil. He looked up at the sky once more as if seeking an answer to his troubles. Then, with a sigh, he turned and went back to bed, unaware of the Guardian perched outside his window.

WEDNESDAY MORNING DAWNED HOT AND sticky. Wil's mom sat at the kitchen bar, sipping coffee. She looked up when he came into the room. The testiness Wil felt only intensified; it was clear his mom had not slept well the night before. Her dark tresses were uncombed, her eyes weak and tinged in pink, as though from crying. When she spoke, her voice sounded tight, as though she was fighting back tears.

"Good morning, honey. How did you sleep?"

"Okay." He dropped his bookbag and moved into the kitchen. As he poured a bowl of cereal, he became aware of Cassia just above his head; she hovered with her legs crossed, invisible to the tired eyes of his mom. She watched cautiously the exchange between mother and son. He looked at her for a moment, but the tension was so great, he could find little pleasure in her presence.

"Good." Nora toyed with an empty sugar packet. "I had a hard time sleeping myself."

Wil kept his back to her; he didn't want to see the look on her face, the look that would mirror the strain in her voice. He heard her slide off the stool.

"Wil, please talk to me." She stood behind him. "This silence isn't helping. I need to know how you feel."

Wil turned past her, keeping his gaze averted. "I'm fine."

"That's what you said after your dad died, that you were 'fine,' always 'fine.' Honey, I'm your mother. I know when you're 'fine' and when you're not. You haven't been 'fine' since Tim passed away."

Wil stirred his cereal with his spoon. The coldness had settled over him again. The nightmare flashed before his mind's eye; his surliness increased.

Nora took a deep breath and tried again. "I told him all about you. He said you … sounded like a neat kid. I told him you were, that your dad and I have always been proud of you. I … I think you should … meet him … when you're ready."

Wil spun around and glared at her. "What? I don't want to meet him! What makes you think that would be okay?"

"I just think it might be helpful if you had a man in your life that you could talk to about things."

"I had one," Wil shot back. "Dad, and he died."

"I know, honey, but—"

"And I thought you said this wasn't a serious thing, or did you lie about that?"

"I don't know." She spread her hands helplessly. "I don't know where this is going, if it's even going anywhere. I just worry about you, honey. You won't talk to me about your dad's death, and it's been three years. I just wonder if you had a male in your life that you would …"

"What? Talk about Dad to a total stranger? No way! No one is ever going to take his place." He stood and grabbed his book-bag.

"Wil, I'm not suggesting a substitution for your dad. No one could ever replace Tim." His mom looked close to tears. He knew this wasn't how she had wanted this conversation to go. He didn't care.

"You want me to meet this guy to give you my approval. Well, it's not going to happen. Go. Be with him! Date him! Sleep with him, if you want to. It's not like the memory of dad is going to stop you!"

She slapped him. Cassia couldn't tell who was more stunned: Nora, who had never struck her son a day in his life, or Wil, who knew deep down he had it coming but couldn't believe it had actually happened.

It was hard to keep the tears from forming in his eyes, but he blinked them back. He turned on his heel before his mom could recover and stomped out of the house. The door slammed behind him. He wiped his eyes, the sting of the slap still burning his cheek.

Scott met him halfway up the walk. He looked tired and pale; faint circles stood out under his eyes, but Wil didn't pay too much attention.

"Whoa! That's a mean look. What's got you in such a bad mood?" Scott stared at his cheek, pink from the punishment.

Wil scowled at him and left the front porch. Scott hurried to catch up with him.

"Seriously, dude. What happened?"

Wil gritted his teeth. "I had a fight with my mom."

"You and your mom?" Scott shook his head, incredulous. "What's that about?"

At that moment, Cassia drifted down beside Wil and fell in step with him.

"Your mother had water leaking from her eyes. What does this mean?" She sounded perplexed.

"She's crying," Wil responded without slowing down.

"Crying?" Scott stopped walking. "Your mom is crying? What did you say to her?"

Wil kept walking, annoyance burning inside him.

"Wil! What the hell did you say to make your mom cry?" Scott sounded indignant.

Wil stopped. The bitterness inside began growing again. He looked up and met the gentle blue eyes of Cassia. Questions hung on her face, but she didn't ask them. He turned towards his friend.

"She told me she met someone, some guy named Larry. They've been going out for a few weeks."

Scott let out a low whistle. "And you got jerky about it, didn't you?"

Wil eyeballed him. "What the hell does that mean? What do you know about it?"

"I know she's your mom, and you made her cry. That's a punk thing to do."

"Oh, I'm sure she'll be okay. She can always talk to *Larry*." He spat the name out of his mouth as the bus came around the corner.

Cassia studied him; the sensations flowing from him were familiar to her. She had felt them quite frequently since taking this assignment, but never had they been *this* strong, *this* fierce.

"What's your problem, Wil? You want your mom to what? Be a hermit? She's a nice lady, and she deserves to have someone take her out every once in a while."

Wil threw down his glove and bookbag and took a couple of steps towards Scott. "Don't start with me, Scott. You wouldn't be so keen on it if it was your mom."

"Your mom *is* the only mom I've ever had, and I think it's good that someone wants to take her out."

"Yeah, provided he's not a drunk." Wil glared at Scott, his hands clenched into fists.

Scott matched his stare. "What, are you going to hit me? Make your descent into ass-holiness final?"

Wil gritted his teeth, every fiber seething with fury. The bus pulled to a stop beside them.

"What's going on here?" asked the bus driver, standing in case he needed to intervene.

Wil and Scott still glared at each other.

"Nothing," Wil finally responded. He turned around and picked up his glove and bag. "I'm walking to school."

Cassia watched him as he headed down the street. She looked back at Scott. Different sensations flowed from him; had she been able to decipher his emotions, she would have sensed disappointment with a touch of disgust. As Scott climbed onto the bus, Cassia hurried to catch up with Wil.

"How do you feel?" she asked as she fell in step beside him.

"I'm fine," Wil retorted.

"No, I do not think you are. This is not usual for—"

"What?" Wil turned on her, impatience etched into his face. "Who are you to tell me what I feel?"

She took a step back; some wild, unknown force oozed from Wil and attacked her sensibilities.

Wil, at seeing her face, took a deep breath. Keeping his voice calm took a lot of effort. "Look, Cassia, I know you have questions, but right now I just need for you to leave me alone."

Cassia felt the internal struggle within him; instinct told her she would never get through the invisible wall that had suddenly appeared.

"Of course." She faded into the familiar wisp of cloud and drifted away. Wil watched her go, a feeling much worse than the cold stone settling over him. He turned on his heel and made the solitary trek to school.

Cassia respected his wishes and left him alone; although she wasn't absent from his day, she did keep herself invisible to him. Wil may not have been able to see her, but the ever-present fragrance of cinnamon apples tickled his nose, annoying him. His irritation grew when Janet sat down next to him, breathless and worried.

"What in the world has happened between you and Scott?" she asked as they worked out of their books. "He sure was sore when he got here this morning, and he all he would say was that you were acting like a punk."

"Scott's a jerk." Wil refused to meet her gaze.

"He's your best friend!" Janet couldn't keep the incredulity out of her voice.

Wil waved her off and slid over into an empty seat. Blindly, he filled in the answers to the sheet he was working on, not caring whether they were right or wrong.

During history, he took his test without even looking at the questions. Cassia lingered at the window. She puzzled over the changing feelings she felt; Wil's hostility began to give way to misery and regret. However, he ignored all of them and waited impatiently for the day to be over.

When it came time to go to lunch, Wil headed for the library. He didn't want to be around his friends, and he especially didn't want to see Scott. The cinnamon aroma lingered several paces behind him; a small part of him wished Cassia would just go back to the clouds, but a much larger part of him wished she would hold his hand again and take away the anger and hurt. She did neither, instead remaining a silent but constant presence.

Wil weaved his way through the throng of students noisily making their way to the cafeteria or to their next class. Someone bumped into him rather painfully.

"Hey, Freak Boy," Andrew sneered, "why don't you watch where you're going?"

"Why don't you?" Wil snapped. It was the second time that day Wil felt any sort of amazement at his actions. Andrew looked downright stunned.

"Well, well," he mocked after a moment, "looks like the Freak has finally gotten a backbone." He poked Wil in the shoulder as a crowd began to gather. "And without your little friends around to protect you, too."

Wil shoved Andrew away from him. "What's the matter? Jealous?"

"Of you, Punk? No way."

"I think you are." Wil shoved Andrew again. A deep, dark sort of pleasure settled in his belly. "I think you can't stand the fact that no one wants to associate with a no-good asshole like you."

Andrew's face darkened. "You think you can do this?" he challenged.

"Anytime you want."

"How about right now?" And Andrew threw a punch that knocked Wil back into the lockers. Wil recovered enough to ward off the next punch, and he retaliated with his own. His fist connected with Andrew's jaw, and a pain shot up his arm. Andrew grabbed him and threw him back into the lockers. The two boys pummeled each other with blows, neither one doing any serious damage as they were too wrapped around each other to make any major hits.

As teachers scrambled to get into the circle to break up the fight, Wil got his fist underneath Andrew and punched. Andrew stumbled back, holding his stomach, his breath cut short. Wil knocked him backwards with a blow to the nose. Standing over him, his fists still curled, his breath coming fast, Wil experienced one moment of complete satisfaction.

Andrew held his hand up to his nose to staunch the blood. His eyes flickered past Wil. He stared for so long, Wil looked over his shoulder; Cassia stood between Stacey Jo and Juan Archuro. She looked startled and dumbfounded, and her gaze was on Andrew.

Wil spun back towards his nemesis, a frown creasing his brow. He looked back at Cassia, and this time, she met his gaze. Wil's sense of pleasure dissipated suddenly. Three teachers forced themselves through the crowd and ordered the students to get to where they needed to be. One of them collected Andrew from the floor, and a second one grabbed Wil by the arm.

Cassia watched them as they were led away. A banshee's shriek filled her ears, invisible but very real. She didn't know how it had happened or how to prevent it from happening again, and she felt weak, drained by the experience.

"It takes many moons to develop the ability to filter out such sensations." Samson's words came back to her as did the rest of the Council's warnings:

"Wil Johnson may very well cast off his innocence after these events. If that happens, the truth of our people may be in jeopardy."

"If that happens, he becomes a very real target for Meslo's corruption."

"But he may very well hold onto his innocence. You are to see that he does. That is why you must be present when these events unfold."

"How am I to help him when I do not understand him?" Cassia asked herself. With a deep breath to steady her senses, she sought an open window. Then she transformed herself and drifted out of the building and into the sky where she could recuperate and find the answers she sought.

WIL'S MOM OPENED THE FRONT door and walked in, her mouth tight with displeasure. Wil followed her into the house and plopped down on the sofa in the den.

"Fighting. At school." She shook her head. "I knew you were upset, but to do this...."

Wil didn't reply; the fight had taken most of his energy, but it was Cassia's expression which had quelled the bitterness inside him. He felt defeated.

"I guess I should be thankful that Principal Banks only suspended you for three days instead of longer. He said due to the fact that this is the first time you have ever been in trouble, he was willing to cut you a break. Still, this is just not like you. Maybe I shouldn't have told you about Larry. Maybe I shouldn't have expected you to deal with this like a responsible person."

Wil closed his eyes to her words. He wanted the world to go away. He wanted the image of Cassia to go away.

The doorbell chimed. Nora sighed and went to open the door. Wil heard her say, "This isn't really a good time, Scott."

"I just figured I could talk to him, Mrs. J."

She let him in and followed him into the den. Wil refused to look at either one of them.

"Good luck," she said to Scott. "If you get anything out of

him, let me know. I've got to get back to work. I'll be late tonight since now I have time to make up." She started out of the room, then stopped.

"I hope you didn't think your little stunt was going to force me to stay locked up in this house. It's been a really long time for me, Wil. I can't stay stationary. I need to move on with my life, not continue to play the part of the grieving widow. Taking this step was the hardest decision I could have made." She looked close to tears again, but at the last moment, she got control. "We can deal with this issue and," her eyes cut to Scott for a moment, "anything else you wish to talk about tomorrow."

"Bye, Mrs. J," Scott said as she walked out of the room. He looked over at Wil, who scowled at him.

"What are you doing here?"

"What are *you* doing, picking a fight with Andrew McGhee? I don't know whether to be proud of you for standing up to that punk or to question your stupidity."

Silence filled the room. Scott sat on the edge of the oversized chair.

"So, what did it feel like, hitting that jerk?"

"It felt like a fight, Scott." An image of Cassia appeared before Wil's eyes. He shut his eyes tightly and rubbed them, willing her to go away. "Why are you here?"

Scott tapped his toes lightly on the rug. "I know you're probably still pissed and everything, but..." Wil cut him a sharp look. "Do you think I can crash here tonight? Dad's been a little depressed this week. It's kind of a downer being there."

"I don't think that's a good idea." Wil got up and walked over to the window. Late afternoon clouds dotted the sky. "My mom's pretty peeved. She's gonna want to have a talk and all that." On the inside, Wil didn't want Scott around; he didn't want anyone around.

Scott nodded, although there was the tiniest flicker of disappointment on his face. "No problem. I can stay in the attic. Dad's moods don't usually reach that high." He stood. "Look, Wil, I'm not gonna tell you how to feel, but your mom hasn't been happy in a really long time. Don't you think it's time for her to be happy again, even if it's not the way you want?"

Wil didn't answer; he continued to stare out at the skyline.

"Right. Well, see you later." Scott left the room, his shoulders slumped.

Wil heard the front door shut. His friend was gone, Cassia was gone, and his mom was disappointed in him. For the first time. And so was he.

He had never felt more miserable in his life.

Chapter 8

Cassia gazed up at the moon hanging low in the sky. She looked over her shoulder into Wil's bedroom; his computer was on and he blindly tapped at the keys, the cartoonish characters running across the screen. His warrior hacked at a giant spider and collected some gold. Wil didn't seem to notice; his expression stayed sorrowful. And bitter. When his character fell into a booby trap, he turned his sad eyes towards the window and rested his chin in his hand.

Cassia considered showing herself to him to help ease his troubles, but she didn't. It wasn't about him right at this moment, and she had a mission to fulfill, one that would affect him, in what way she knew not.

The computer beeped, and Wil turned his attention back to his game. Cassia turned hers back to the moon. A darkness settled over her.

"When seven moons have passed, you must go to this shelter."

Jereni's voice stirred Cassia from her perch outside Wil's window. Silently, Cassia faded into the wispy mist of cloud and drifted above the sleeping houses. A couple of blocks over from Wil's house, she spotted the "shelter" she was to be at. A window on the bottom floor was open. She slid through it, allowing her human form to take over as her feet touched the floor.

Something cold and threatening took hold of her. She looked around, seeking the source. This shelter was similar to Wil's; the room she was in now was some sort of den, though newspapers, magazines, and junk mail littered the floor and the coffee table. There hung on the air a stale stench, like mildew and beer. On the coffee table sat empty food containers and an upturned glass, whose contents had puddled on the corner and trickled down the leg. A votive candle burned openly in a saucer dish. On the two end tables were more little glasses and some empty bottles with labels that read "Jim Bean" and "Captain Jack." Two other candles burned, in an obvious effort to drown out the stench with their scents: one on an end table and one on the mantle, their flames still in the motionless room.

Cassia stared at them; the threatening feeling intensified, and she puzzled harder. Suddenly, she became aware of shouting from the next room. Drifting slowly across the room, she peered around the door frame. Scott was pinned against the wall by a man three times his age. The man might have been attractive but for the drunken rage contorting his face.

"Where the hell is the money?" he yelled at Scott, who blanched even while he pushed against the man's arm.

"I don't have any more," Scott replied, struggling. "You drank it all away."

"You lying son-of-a-bitch." The man tossed Scott into the kitchen counter. The weak light from overhead threw shadows around the two, but when Scott turned his face to follow the footsteps of the man, Cassia saw clearly the bruise on his cheek.

The man grabbed Scott's bookbag and turned it upside down. Scott watched silently as the books and notebooks tumbled out amid other stuff: his locker key, a deck of cards, his video games, a bus ticket for a town several hundred miles away.

"What the hell's this?" the man demanded, holding up the ticket. "A bus ticket? What the hell do you need with a bus ticket?" He came towards Scott, the ticket gripped in his hand. "Is this where you spent the money? On some lousy, no good bus ticket?" He grabbed Scott by the collar.

"Dad," Scott pleaded, "you're drunk."

"Don't you tell me what I am!" the man raged. He shook Scott, tossed him aside, then slapped him into the wall. Scott fell at Cassia's feet; she watched, horrified, as Scott touched his fingers to his mouth. When he pulled his hand away, blood showed on his finger. The horror inside Cassia began to change rapidly to anger. When his dad jerked him off the floor, Scott punched him in the jaw. The blow caught his dad off guard, and he released Scott. Scott ran from the room, right past Cassia, up the steps to the attic where he slammed and bolted the door shut.

"Lousy, no-good, son-of-a-bitch!" his dad yelled after him before stumbling to the refrigerator. He pulled out a six pack of beer and staggered to the couch. Sitting down, he popped open a can, threw his feet up on the coffee table, and guzzled the beer.

Cassia left him to his drink and floated out the open window to the one on the upper floor. Scott sat on a pallet on the floor, the anguish evident on his face. He studied a picture in his hand, a picture of Wil and him on the basketball court, t-shirts damp with sweat, hair matted to their heads, goofy grins on their faces.

Scott sighed and set the picture down. He wiped his mouth with the back of his hand and touched his tender cheek, already purple. He thumped his head deliberately against the wall, and a great anguish filled Cassia. She watched as he slid down and rolled over. As he shut his eyes, a lone tear trickled down the bridge of his nose.

Cassia struggled to close herself off to the onslaught of emotions. The darkness she had felt earlier had swelled and diminished with the fight; however, the threat that accompanied that overwhelming darkness still grew, little by little, beat by beat. Cassia wasn't sure what would come of it, but she knew that she had to wait for it to peak. She had to be here if she was to truly help Wil.

The moon climbed higher in the sky, and still the threat grew. Scott slept, weary and sad, on the pallet. Cassia waited in the dark, fighting against the crushing sadness, fear, and anger she didn't understand. Her instincts prickled with the sinister shadows, and she held out her hand. The magical orb appeared, glowing in pale blue light. She held it up to her face and peered into it.

The scene from downstairs came into view. Scott's dad sat on the couch, his eyes bleary red, staring at nothing. Six empty beer cans littered the coffee table and the couch. He held up the bus ticket and gazed at it, his unfocused eyes not seeing anything. After a moment, he stumbled up, catching himself on the coffee table. His hand knocked the candle over onto a stack of envelopes. Oblivious to the black spot spreading across the top envelope, he staggered to the front door. Mumbling to himself about the lousy lot in his life, he wrenched the door open and lurched out into the night.

Cassia watched in guarded fascination as the flame spread over the top paper and found incentive to keep living in the liquor puddled on the table.

The fire traveled from the puddle to the newspaper lying next to it, then to the magazines, the coupons, the advertisements, the bills, the solicitations; from the top of the blazing table top fell a burning piece of paper; other periodicals were seized by the happy flames, spreading more and more quickly across the floor, to the end table, to the chair, to the curtains, up the walls towards the ceilings.

A streak of flame lapped greedily at the fabric of the couch. A second streak consumed an end table, a third streak the doorway to the kitchen.

Cassia heard the joyous cry of the fire as the paint peeled away and the wood began to groan in agony. The flames spread out, seeking more life-giving substances.

Cassia waved her hand and the orb vanished. Her eyes darted to the door bolted against the known human demon; she knew such a barrier would not stop the unknown fiend climbing towards them.

She moved to stand beside Scott, who was lost in a miserable sleep. Smoke, gray and new in its awakenings, began to seep into the room. Outside the attic door, Cassia could hear the celebratory roar of the flames as they surged towards them.

Concentrating all her effort on the figure lying at her feet, she spoke.

"Scott, you need to awaken."

There was no movement, no indication that he had heard her.

"There is danger approaching."

Still no movement, no sign that her voice had reached human ears. The smoke grew thicker, blacker; the heat radiated through the floor.

Cassia focused her energies. "Scott, it is Cassia. You must hear me. You *must* awaken now."

A shrill whine drifted in through the windows. Stepping over to the window, Cassia saw flashing red lights approaching. Human voices floated up to meet her ears: worried, frightened calls from one neighbor to another as they were awakened by the approaching lights and noise.

The attic door groaned as the flames pushed through it. Facing the fire, Cassia heard the laughter, the pleasure, it took in its destruction. She moved near Scott again and concentrated.

"Scott, it is Cassia. Come with me. Danger is very close."

Scott shifted in his sleep but did not awaken. Smoke swirled around the room, smothering the pure air with a vengeance. Like a giant claw, it made its way towards Scott and Cassia. The flames followed behind, not as eager as they took their time to feast on the wood and cardboard boxes stacked in the corner.

Cassia stood stoically against the smoke; it roiled about her, furious that it could not bring her to her knees. But the flames knew her weakness, knew how to penetrate the defenses of Olin; they sent their heat at her, wave after wave. She fought to maintain control; she had to find a way to reach Scott, but the intensifying heat began to drain her. The fear and concern from the humans congregated below attacked her sensibilities. Scott's sadness and anger beat at her, weakening her abilities.

"Scott." The attic grew red with the flames, creeping closer and closer. Heat swelled the room. Smoke masked everything.

"Scott." Cassia fell to her knees; the flames leaped with laughter, some of them landing on the beams overhead, some of them spreading out like human fingers towards her, towards the pallet.

Cassia reached out a hand and tried to grasp Scott's arm; her hand passed right through him. A flame lapped at her, grazing her arm. She stared at the blue-red surrounding Scott before fading into her natural state and disappearing out the window.

Wil walked downstairs. The clock on the wall showed 2:27 a.m., but he hadn't been able to sleep. After playing the game for several hours, he had tried reading, but even the world of fantasy couldn't lift him from his dejection. He hadn't been able to shake Cassia's expression out of his mind, and he regretted having spoken to her the way he did. He regretted many things, things that were all his fault, things that only he could make right. The night seemed a lot darker without the promise of Scott and Cassia in tomorrow's light. The idea that it was his fault they wouldn't be there left him feeling numb, unable to concentrate on any one task.

So, he had tried putting his faith in the old cliché that tomorrow would be better and sleeping, but it hadn't come easily; when it had finally settled over him, sirens had awakened him. He had looked out his window to see if he could determine what was going on. The cloudless night sky had depressed him, and he had come downstairs for a midnight snack.

Opening the refrigerator door, he poked around the shelves and at a couple of containers before settling on leftover pasta salad. He shut the door and turned around. She stood in front of him, her face pallid, her blue eyes pained.

"Cassia!" The relief that washed over Wil was so immediate it took him a moment to recognize her distress. He set down the pasta container and grabbed her hands without thinking. "What's wrong?"

Sensations pummeled Wil with fierceness, sensations to which he was familiar: anger, sadness, hurt, distress ... and fear.

Wil stared at her. "Why are you afraid?" The cold stone settled in his stomach again.

"*I* am not." Being in human form was very difficult, but she knew she had to be here. The Council's warning had been stringent and direct.

"Then what—" Just then, the doorbell chimed. Wil spun towards the door, but he didn't let go of her hands. "What's going on?" He turned back towards her. The look on her face was not comforting.

The doorbell chimed again, and then someone knocked on the door. Wil didn't move. The rustle of his mother's footsteps on the stairs was heard. She opened the door, and Wil heard murmured voices.

"*Why are you afraid?*" Wil demanded again.

She shook her head and whispered, "It is not my fear you are sensing."

The feeling washed over him, transferred from her being to his instinctively.

"Scott." His whisper hung unanswered in the air. Cassia merely looked at him, the stress of the excessive emotion on her face. Wil let go of her hands and walked slowly around the kitchen doorway. At the end of the hallway stood his mother. The front door was open, and as Wil made his way towards it, he could see a fireman framed in the doorway. He stopped talking as Wil approached. Behind him, a police car flashed its blue lights in the blackness of night, a police officer standing by the car.

Nora turned towards her son, tears streaking her cheeks. She wiped them away and took his hand.

Wil stared at the fireman. His face was handsome with a weathered, experienced look. His green eyes met Wil's.

"Wil, honey," Nora said, struggling to keep her voice steady. "There's, um, there's been an accident."

Wil waited. The cold stone grew leaps and bounds; his stomach felt like an ice pit. He continued to stare at the fireman.

"There was a ... fire, and, um, well ..."

Wil looked at his mother. "It was Scott, wasn't it." His voice sounded calm, detached. Inside, he felt frozen, dead.

She nodded and new tears threatened to fall as she answered him. "It's not good."

Wil turned his attention back to the fireman as he spoke.

"They've taken him to the hospital for smoke inhalation. There are some minor burns to his body, but the major concern is the smoke." He glanced at Nora as he talked. "He was unresponsive at the scene, but the paramedics were able to get him breathing again en route to the hospital. He also had some bruises on his body, his cheek and his lip. Officer Monroe will talk to you about that, so if either of you know anything ...?"

Nora shook her head silently. Wil recalled Scott sitting on the edge of the chair in his living room: *"I can stay in the attic. Dad's moods don't usually reach that high."*

"His dad," Wil mumbled, his eyes unable to leave the face of the fireman. "He drinks, so ..." His mother shot him a look as his voice trailed off. The fireman nodded, his face grave with the seriousness of the situation.

"Officer Monroe can drive you both to the hospital if you'd like," he offered.

"Oh, yes. Yes, we should go." Nora turned away from the door.

"How did you know to come here?" Wil asked suddenly. His mother stopped fussing with her purse and keys.

The fireman pulled a picture out of the back of his notebook and handed it to Wil. "The paramedics found this by his bed. I asked some of the neighbors if they knew the identity of the second boy in the picture, and they told me where to find you."

Wil stared at the picture. *"I can stay in the attic. Dad's moods don't usually reach that high."*

"Here, honey." His mother passed him a pair of sweatpants and his jacket from the hall closet. She threw her jacket on over her bathrobe. Taking her son's arm, she steered him out of the house and into the police car. Wil continued to stare at the picture as the police car pulled away from the curb.

A SOFT LIGHT GLOWED IN the hospital room. Underneath the pale illumination lay Scott, unconscious. Oxygen tubes were fitted into his nose, and the IV tube ran a continual liquid into the vein on the back of his hand. His left arm and leg were bandaged; so was his right foot.

Wil stood at the bedside, staring down at his friend. The bruise on Scott's face stood out ghastly against the ashy whiteness. The cut on his swollen lip was pink with freshness.

"Severe amount of smoke intake… is in a comatose state… if he regains consciousness, there could be some brain damage… all we can do now is wait…"

The doctor's words rang hollowly in Wil's ears. *"If he regains consciousness…"* The words had followed him into Scott's room; they echoed and bounced off the walls. *"If he regains consciousness…"*

His mother came up behind him, her hand on his shoulder a familiar and comforting gesture.

"I'm so sorry, sweetheart," she whispered. "To think that's our Scott…" Wil continued to gaze at him.

"I can't believe this is happening," Nora continued quietly. "Scott is always so lively, it's really hard seeing him like this." She moved to the end of the bed. "I knew something was wrong. Why didn't he tell us, tell *me*?" Her hand massaged her temple. "I was going to go by there this weekend. It's just this job I've been trying for…" She sniffled. "Stupid, lousy job. Why didn't I go? He must have been so frightened." She rubbed at her temple again, tears threatening to fall. They didn't, though, and when she spoke, her voice was steadier. "The house was completely destroyed, so I'm going to take off work tomorrow and see if I can put together some things for him, some clothes. I need to call the school about his textbooks, see if I can get some extra copies so when he returns to school—"

"Mom?" Wil looked at her, and she stopped her ramble. "I want to go home."

Nora watched him carefully and nodded. She crossed over to Scott and bent down to kiss his forehead. For a moment, Wil thought she might cry again, and he willed her not to. He needed to get out of this room, this hospital, this place of healing that had taken his dad three years ago and now threatened to take his friend. He thought he might be sick.

She stood up and took her son's hand. They walked out of the room and found Officer Monroe standing at the nurse's station.

"We would like to go home," she said. The officer nodded wordlessly and escorted them out of the hospital.

Once home, Wil slowly climbed the steps to his bedroom while his mother thanked the cop for his assistance. After shutting his bedroom door, Wil rested his head against it, the truth of the last few hours washing over him. *Why didn't he tell us?… He must have been so scared.* The words pounded at him like a sledge hammer. *Why didn't he tell me?*

Why didn't you listen?

Wil turned around and saw her standing there, her lovely form outlined by the morning sun that was just now beginning to rise. Without hesitating, Wil marched over to her and grabbed her hands. He felt the anger and sadness flood him again, only this time there was no fear, no distress, no hurt.

"It was Scott's fear, wasn't it?" he demanded, a fierce energy surging though his weary body.

She nodded, her blue eyes less luminous than usual, but still calm.

"All of this," he held up her hands as though she needed proof of what he was talking about, "belongs to Scott. The feelings were his."

She nodded again, still silent. The surge of emotions emanating from Wil assaulted her, but she maintained control.

Wil dropped her hands and backed away from her. A frown creased his forehead. "You were there, weren't you? You were at his house."

A third nod.

"Say something!" Wil exploded. She blanched as though she had been hit. With a deep breath, she struggled to settle the emotional attack.

"Yes, I was."

"And you did nothing!"

Fury wrapped itself around her.

"There was nothing I could do. Scott cannot hear me or see me, not like I am."

"You could have stopped the fire. Isn't that what your people do?"

"No. This was not Meslo's doing. This was a human fire caused by a human. I cannot intervene in the actions of man."

Rage clawed at her; impatience tugged at the cords of her essence; misery threatened to suffocate her.

"He could have died!" Wil shouted at her, lost in his antipathy. "He might already be dead! Don't you care about that?"

"Of course I do." The calmness in her voice irritated him all the more.

"Then why didn't you try? You did nothing. You came to me when it was already too late. Why? *Why are you here?*"

"I told you, Wil, I am here for you."

He grabbed her by the arms. She gasped as the final fury constricted its grip on her soul. Unshed tears burned in Wil's eyes; his grip on her tightened.

"*I* don't need you! Scott needed you! You should have been here for him. You should have done something!"

"Wil—" Her faint voice couldn't meet his ears.

"Did you see his dad hit him? Did you watch his dad drink himself into a rage?" His fingers dug into her arms; his rage dug into her essence. She struggled to maintain her human shape.

"His dad got out, but not Scott. Why didn't you help Scott? *Why* didn't you get him out of the house?"

Cassia didn't reply. Wil dropped his head, his hold on her relaxing. He turned away from her, his shoulders slumped with sorrow and fatigue.

"Get out."

His quiet voice, so sudden from the shouting, caught her off guard. So, too, did the pain reverberating through her human body. She staggered against the window.

Wil turned towards her, his eyes distant, his voice cold. "Go away. I don't need you here." The pain shook her again. "Leave me alone."

Cassia could not contain the agony. The last sight she saw was the banshee crawling in through the window, her red lips glinting over her fangs. She shrieked laughter as Cassia's essence split, and her human form was shattered. The mist hung in the air for but a moment, then disappeared out the window.

Wil pulled the picture from his jacket pocket; Scott's goofy grin stared back at him. Wil moved to his computer desk, a false calm hanging about him. He set the picture against one of his books, then swiped at the rest of his books. They tumbled into the floor. The violent gesture felt good, the release of energy upon inanimate objects; Wil turned towards his book shelf and hurled books across the room. He grabbed at the Harry Potter poster hanging on his wall and ripped it, once, twice, three times. He kicked at his night stand and sent the lamp crashing to the floor; he upset his mattress and knocked the picture of his dad and him playing baseball onto the floor.

The noise brought his mom rushing up the steps. She flung open the door and gaped at her son, who had crumpled into his computer chair, his head held in his hands.

"Wil, what on earth …?"

He looked up at her, tears streaking his cheeks. His voice cracked as he spoke. "It's my fault, mom. It's all my fault Scott's in the hospital."

"No." She knelt beside him, stunned and relieved to see the emotion on his face. "It was an accident."

Wil refused to be comforted. He shook his head. "He wanted to stay here this weekend. He asked, but I said no because I was angry with him because he said you should be going out and I didn't want to hear what he said, I didn't want to hear what anybody said, so I said no and he was asleep in the attic when he could have been here where it was safe, but I said no, Mom. Why did I say no?"

He fell into her arms and cried on her shoulder. "Shhh." She stroked his hair to quiet his emotional ramble. "It's not your fault, Wil. This was a terrible, terrible tragedy. But you have to have faith that Scott is going to get better. You have to believe that."

Wil sat back and wiped his eyes. "It didn't help Dad."

Nora looked away for a moment. When she met her son's anguished gaze, she looked strong, confident, though sad.

"No, it didn't. But Scott is not your father, and he has a very good chance of surviving."

Wil resisted giving in to her comfort. "And what if he doesn't? I helped put him in there. If I wouldn't have been such a jerk, he would be here right now. He would be safe, not lying in a bed with tubes sticking out of him."

"Scott's a pretty tough kid. If anybody can beat this, he can."

Wil shook his head and looked up at the pictures hanging crookedly on the wall. "I miss Dad. He should be here, too."

"Yes." Her quiet voice drew his attention. Tears rimmed her eyes, but she swallowed them. "And yet life goes on somehow, and if we are to be fair to your dad's memory, then we have to make sure we live the life that he didn't get a chance to."

Wil sniffed and wiped his eyes with the back of his hand. "I'm sorry I've been such a jerk lately. The things I said to you—"

She shook her head and cupped his distressed face in her hands. "Honey, it's all right. We both got a little carried away. I know it hasn't been easy for you. But I think now... you're gonna be all right." She looked him square in the face. "And so is Scott."

Wil wanted to believe her. He looked around at the destruction of his room. "I guess I'd better clean up this mess."

"Never mind that now. Why don't you get a shower, and I'll make us something to eat?" Nora stood.

"Scott likes your cooking."

"Well, then, we'll just have to make sure we take him some dinner when he wakes up." She smiled encouragement at him, but her eyes betrayed her concern. Wil decided to make it easier on her; he nodded and stood.

She moved to his doorway and paused, watching him. When he looked at her, she smiled a genuine smile. "I love you, Wil."

The first stirrings of calm began to settle over him.

"I love you, too, Mom."

Chapter 9

Wil spent the afternoon at the hospital. His mom had dropped him off on her way to run some errands, errands that focused solely on Scott's awakening. Wil silently admired the way his mother refused to be held down by grief or pessimism. He remembered the days and weeks following his dad's death; his mom had somehow found the strength to call the funeral home and make arrangements, see to Wil's dinner and grief, pick out an appropriate suit for burial, greet other grieving family members at the wake, see to the insurance papers, handle the finances, and keep the carpet vacuumed. It was only in the quiet privacy of the night tucked inside her bedroom that she released her own grief. Wil guessed the old adage about keeping busy to keep one's mind off of things was true, though he didn't know where she found the energy. He was exhausted from his emotional outburst.

Scott slept peacefully, his bruises and bandages betrayers of the truth. The only sound in the room was the steady beep from his IV machine, which also provided some pain medication in case Scott could feel any through his deep slumber.

Wil stood from the chair he had been sitting in for the last hour. He walked over to the window and raised the blinds. The afternoon was sunny and warm, the bright blue sky free of any clouds. Wil watched the skies for nearly a half-hour, but no clouds appeared. Turning with a sigh, he picked up a magazine that lay nearby and flipped through it three times before his mom arrived to take him home. He slept on the couch that night, too tired to deal with the ruin of his room.

The next morning, Wil arose and went for a walk. The spring morning felt cool and comforting on his face. The sky above him was again free of clouds and shone deep blue. Wil let his feet carry him nearly two blocks before he became conscious of his surroundings. Yellow police tape wrapped around the whole of the property; in the center sat a black and gray frame, completely gutted and without any other support around it. The windows had blown out or melted in the blaze, and soot streaked the frame of the house. Behind the frame, Wil could make out a pile of debris and ash.

He stood there for quite some time, imagining what it must have been like to be trapped inside that inferno. He didn't feel panicked or threatened; he didn't get sick or angry. Looking at this scene brought him no inner turmoil; instead, he felt enlightened in some way that he couldn't describe.

He left the spot only once the sun got too hot to stand still. The irony of it wasn't lost on him as he made his way home. He spent the afternoon cleaning his room, re-hanging pictures, straightening the mattress and making his bed, sweeping up the broken lamp, collecting all the books and re-shelving them. One book in particular caught his attention, and he sat down on the bed, staring at the cover. A small smile pulled at the corners of his lips and he set the book down on the nightstand so he wouldn't forget it.

On Monday, Wil went to the hospital first thing. He spent the day sitting by Scott's bedside, mostly thinking. It seemed a year had passed since Wednesday when his world tipped upside down, but it had only been six days. His mom had been more like a ghost the last few days, flitting in and out of the hospital room, in and out of the house, her actions and locations a mystery. Ever since their talk, she had left her son to himself as much as he needed, a fact he was grateful for. There were so many things to think through, so many emotions to sort and deal with, and the whole business was very tiring.

When Wil left the hospital that day, the nurse informed him that Scott's vital signs were looking much better. He thanked her for the information but didn't place too much hope on it. He didn't think he could take another disappointment.

That night, he stood in front of his window. He secured the blinds up so the moonless night sky peeked in. Pushing open the window, he leaned on the sill and gazed upwards. Millions of stars bedecked the black blanket overhead. No clouds.

Wil sighed. No clouds, no Cassia—something else that had been his doing.

"I'm sorry," he whispered to the giant tree outside his window. The leaves rustled slightly in the breeze. Wil gazed down at the ground without really seeing it. "Please come back."

Only the stars heard his whispers. He turned away and lay down in bed, facing the open window, just in case ...

TUESDAY MORNING, WIL ROSE EARLY and dressed. He was to return to school today, and he wasn't looking forward to it. Not because he worried over what anyone might say about him and the fight (if anyone was still talking about it), but because Scott wouldn't be there. School was interesting because of Scott's flirtations, the rejections, the teasing, the failure to complete an assignment. Without his friend there, Wil knew the day would be long.

He walked into science class and handed Mr. Golden his make-up work.

"Thank you, Mr. Johnson. It's good to have you back."

Wil nodded and took his seat. Janet bustled in, digging through her science book for some lost note. She started in surprise at seeing Wil in his usual seat and threw her books down before grabbing him in a hug.

"Oh, Wil, thank goodness you're back. I've missed you so much."

"Uh, Janet?"

"It's just so terrible about Scott. Everyone's been so upset about it, and I've been worried about you, getting suspended for fighting—"

"Janet? Choking."

She released him suddenly. "Sorry," she said sheepishly. "But really, how are you?"

"Okay." For some reason, he almost felt like he meant it this time.

"Good." She smiled, and Wil noticed for the first time the dimple in her right cheek. "I've been having to work with Juan. You think you suck at science? Pssh!" She shook her head to show how bad it had been.

"Sorry. I'm back now, and I promise I will not let you down again."

"You better not." She shook a playful fist at him as Mr. Golden began to address the class.

First period ended with Wil feeling better than he thought he would. Janet's devotion to their friendship reminded him that though his world had gotten very tipsy the last few days, some things seemed to remain constant.

Second period put him in the library with a substitute. Wil tucked his make-up assignments into his bookbag, knowing better than to give them to the sub. He completed the lessons out of the book in record time, then stood to browse the shelves. Most of his classmates were goofing off, their textbooks closed in front of them; the substitute read the newspaper at a table in the corner.

Wil retreated to the bookcase on the far side of the room, seeking solace. So far, the day had been fairly smooth, but he still wasn't ready to be a part of any discussions concerning Scott.

He started down the last aisle, browsing the titles. A figure in a second-hand black jacket knelt in the middle of the aisle, his hand on a book. He pulled it off the shelf and stood. Wil looked up as the figure turned, and let out an exasperated sigh.

Andrew glared at him. Wil glanced down at the book in his hand: *New Moon* by Stephenie Meyer.

"It's good," Wil said without being asked. "More about Jacob and less about Edward, and the ending is pretty awesome."

"What would I know about it?" Andrew demanded, laying the book on a nearby shelf and shoving past Wil.

Without turning around, Wil made a guess that he knew was right with or without confirmation.

"You see her, don't you?"

Behind him, Andrew stopped. "Who?"

Wil turned slowly, deliberately. "Cassia."

"Of course I see her, Queer Fish. She's in class."

"That's not what I mean. You *see* her the way she really is."

Andrew walked up on him until their faces were inches apart.

"I'm not a freak like you. I don't see pixies and leprechauns in the cafeteria."

Wil held up his hands in surrender and watched as Andrew walked away a second time.

"She's real, you know."

Andrew stopped a second time and stood with his back to Wil for a long time. Finally, he spoke, his voice uncertain, soft.

"She glows."

"Yeah."

"And she floats?" Andrew looked at him to see if Wil was making fun of him. He wasn't.

"Yeah."

"And she turns into..." he shrugged as he searched for the right word, "mist?"

"Cloud, actually."

Andrew stood at a loss for what to say, perplexed. "What does that mean?"

"I don't know." Wil privately grieved at her absence, but kept his face neutral in the presence of his nemesis.

Andrew took a couple of tentative steps towards him. "That day in English class, she was so bright, so glow-y, I thought I had gone crazy."

"Me, too." Wil smiled at the memory. "Especially when nobody else seemed to notice."

Andrew still puzzled over this realization. "And she always smells so sweet, like—"

"Cinnamon apples." They spoke the words together and stared at one another. Wil wondered at the strangeness of this whole situation. He picked up the book and passed it to Andrew.

"Here you go. Don't give up on it."

Andrew stared at the book in his hands and spoke to Wil's retreating back.

"My mom used to tell me these stories when I was little."

Wil stopped and turned around. He waited patiently as Andrew continued.

"She loved fairy tales and princesses and little fairy godmothers." A small smile pulled at the corners of Andrew's mouth. "I don't think she ever grew out of them. She was always looking for a happy ending. I probably knew every tale by the Grimm Brothers before I started kindergarten. She used to tell me, 'Magic is everywhere, Andrew, everywhere.' I was a stupid kid." Sadness crossed his face for a second. "I believed her. I guess some part of me still does. That's why I keep reading these books. I'm looking for the magic. I'm looking for my mom."

Andrew stared at the book in his hand. Then, as if realizing he had said way too much, he looked up, a frown creasing his forehead.

Wil studied him. "What happened to her?"

"And why is that any of your business?" The hostility was returning.

"Because I lost my dad three years ago to cancer. He told me something similar, and that's why I keep reading those books. I was looking for the magic, too, but the magic found me instead. And now my best friend is in the hospital, and I know there's nothing in those pages to help him. There's just me."

Andrew studied him, gauging his sincerity. "My mom died when I was six. Car crash."

"What about your dad?"

Andrew scoffed. "Who knows? He was a drunk. He used to beat my mom, so one night, she packed me up in the car and drove away. She changed her name and gave me her maiden name. He never came looking for us, so when she died, I became a ward of the state. Nice, huh?"

Wil considered his enemy and realized that, for some reason, it was wrong to see Andrew in that light; that somehow, the nature of their relationship was beginning to change.

"That's tough."

Andrew shook his head. "I got these." He held up the book. "And seeing Cassia has helped, too. It's renewed my belief in my mom's words. It may not help your friend, but I'll keep looking, all the same."

Wil nodded as the bell ending class rang. Both boys seem to shake out of their reverie.

"Well, I got to get to lunch. See you in English."

Andrew stared at him; a semi-pleased expression danced across his face. "Yeah, see ya."

Wil crossed the room and picked up his bookbag. Slinging it over his shoulder, he glanced out the large window. Still cloudless.

But not hopeless, he thought with a quick peek at Andrew on the far side of the room. Andrew had settled into a chair and was reading.

Wil allowed himself to get caught up in the throng of students moving towards the cafeteria.

———

"AND THAT'S THE WHOLE STORY." Wil sat back and stared at Scott. His friend still lay unconscious, the tubes still attached to him. "You know, in a funny way, Andrew really isn't that bad of a guy. It's funny how alike we are. I mean, he likes to read and he lost a parent." He paused. "Who knows? One day, we might even be friends."

The afternoon had been rather surreal following the episode with Andrew. Wil's friends had been pleasantly enthusiastic at his return; Stacey Jo and Laurie both hugged him until he was sure his lips had turned blue from near suffocation. Chris and Derek wanted to know details about the fight but respected Wil's dismissal of the event. Somehow, talking about Andrew in that way felt wrong, so the conversation naturally turned to Scott.

Wil listened as his friends worried and hoped. He kept his thoughts quiet, though he was beginning to relinquish some of the guilt he had about that night. He couldn't help glancing at the high windows; he knew there were no clouds, but he halfway believed that if he kept looking hard enough, she would appear. She didn't, and for the first time, he felt a tiny inkling that she might be gone for good.

In English class, Andrew had paused at Wil's desk. He looked as if he wanted to say something, but instead, he merely nodded before moving to his seat at the back of the class. Derek had gawked and turned to Stacey Jo for an explanation; she merely shrugged. Laurie had followed Andrew all the way to his seat with her eyes and smiled at him when he sat. She gave Wil an "I-told-you-so" look, and he nodded to show her she was right. Scott's seat was empty, however, and Wil had to work hard not to stare at it.

After school, Wil had come straight to the hospital. Derek and Laurie had come with him and visited for about an hour. Once they left, Wil, feeling a nervous energy left over from the day, had started talking. He was sure Scott couldn't hear a word he said (although the nurse had told him differently), but he wanted to hear the words spoken out loud; it made it seem more realistic that way.

He had left out everything about Cassia, except to say that she had left and probably wouldn't be back. Unfortunately, that sounded too realistic and filled him with a lonely sadness.

He leaned forward and rested his elbows on his knees. "Look, um, Scott, I know you probably can't hear this, but I'm gonna say it anyway. I was a jerk to you, and I'm sorry. It's kind of my fault you're in here; it's kind of my fault a lot of stuff happened." A memory of Cassia's pained face filled his mind. He shook it off. "Anyway, I wanted to let you know I'm really sorry I acted like I did. You're my best friend, and it's gonna be real hard if you don't pull through."

Wil sat for a second longer before standing and moving towards the window. He gazed at the blue sky, wondering if he would ever get the chance to say the same to Cassia.

"Boy, am I glad that's over."

Wil started and spun around. Scott gazed up at him, mock seriousness on his face.

"Mushy stuff like that belongs in a chick flick."

"Oh my god! You're awake!" Wil stepped over to the bed, elation washing over him.

"Not for long if you keep spouting sentimentality at me."

"When did this happen? Do the nurses know?"

Scott nodded, still groggy. "I guess about lunch time. What day is it?"

"Tuesday." Wil grinned at him. "You've been the talk of the school for the last four days."

Scott grinned, though his eyes were closed. "Cool. A cele-brit-tee."

"Definitely."

Scott opened his eyes and peered at Wil. "You know, I don't really remember much of anything about that night, other than my dad yelling at me. Typical, right?" He mused over something silently. "But there was something else. Maybe I'm crazy, inhaled too much smoke or something, but I would swear I heard someone, a girl, telling me to wake up and get out, that danger was coming."

Wil stared at him. "You heard a girl's voice?"

Scott looked up a bit sheepishly. "'Course, it could have just been a dream. They keep giving me stuff." He lifted his hand with the IV unit in it.

Wil silently kicked himself as the truth began to dawn on him. "Did you … see what she looked like?"

"Nope, although when I think about it, she kind of favors Nina Selna. I don't suppose she's come to cry over my injuries?"

Wil shook his head. "Afraid not, but Derek and Laurie were here a little while ago. You must have really been asleep."

"Or faking it." Again Scott looked sheepish. "I knew if they knew I was awake, they would have stayed, and we wouldn't be able to talk."

Wil grinned at his friend. "Jerk."

Scott grinned back. "Punk." He toyed with the corner of the blanket laying over him. "So you and Andrew have what? Become friends?"

Wil shrugged. "I don't know if that's the right word, but I do think we're not enemies anymore, if we ever were."

"This is just too bizarre, even with the drugs. What brought about his moment of decency?"

An image of Cassia flitted across Wil's mind. He shoved it aside. "I don't know. Maybe the fight?"

"Oh, yeah! You stood up to him! Bullies hate that; it forces them to respect you, or at least leave you alone. I never understood why he was so focused on you. I mean, you must have offended him in another life."

"No, I don't think that was it." Wil grew thoughtful. "I think … he's just lonely. He doesn't really have any friends."

Scott scoffed. "Can you blame anybody for that? I mean, he isn't exactly a ray of sunshine."

Wil studied his friend for a moment and spoke quietly. "He's got a lot in common with you, too, Scott. It's just he has a different way of handling it."

Scott stared at him, a scowl pulling his eyebrows together. Just then, the nurse's aide came in, a tray of food in her hands. "Here you go, Scott, fresh and hot." She set the tray down and removed the lid. Mashed potatoes, macaroni-and-cheese, and meatloaf stared up at him from the plate. A small container of pudding sat beside the plate, along with a milk carton, a piece of bread, and glass of tea.

"Eat up. I'll be back later to take your tray." She left, and Scott grimaced.

"One good reason never, *ever* to land in the hospital."

"You must seriously be sick not to have an appetite," Wil teased him.

"Not sick. Injured, and as such, I should be treated to ice cream."

Wil chuckled and picked up his bag. "Well, I'd better be getting home. Mom'll have dinner waiting."

"Oh, yeah, sure. Rub it in." Scott pouted at the meatloaf in front of him.

"I'll come back tomorrow, and I'll bring you a pizza," Wil promised.

"Supreme, extra cheese."

"You got it, buddy." Wil crossed the room and paused in the doorway. "Scott? I really am glad you're awake."

Scott made a face. "Eww, I can only deal with one nauseating thing at a time."

Wil grinned and left Scott puzzling over the meatloaf on his tray.

"I'm home, Mom!"

Wil laid his bookbag in the front hallway and followed his happy nose down the hall. He poked his head in the kitchen; a lasagna casserole sat cooling on a trivet. Two bowls of salad were on the table beside two plates and two glasses of tea. A basket of garlic bread sat on the counter.

"I'm upstairs!" his mom called back.

Wil picked up the basket and placed it on the table. He pulled off a piece of bread and trotted up the steps. His mom stood in the hallway near the guest bedroom, a preoccupied expression on her face.

"Hey, mom. Dinner smells great. Scott is going to be sooo jealous."

She smiled. "Did you see him then? I called the hospital this afternoon, and they told me he was awake."

"Yeah, it's great. I told him I'd bring him a pizza tomorrow, but I might take him some of your lasagna. Something tells me that would make him happier. He loves your cooking." He popped the piece of bread into his mouth.

"Really?" That seemed to please her for a moment. Her expression turned anxious again. "Wil, has Scott given any thought to after he gets out of the hospital? Where he's going to go?"

The piece of bread seemed to get stuck in his throat. He forced it down. "No, I don't think he …" What was it Andrew had said? A ward of the state? Suddenly, Wil didn't feel so well.

"Well, how would you feel if he came to stay with us for a little while?" Nora continued, pushing open the guest room door. Wil peered inside. The bed was neatly made, the comforter showing signs of a good cleaning. The floor had been vacuumed and new curtains hung in the window. On the bed were a new iPod, a new pair of shoes, and a new baseball mitt. On the desk sat two new notebooks, a set of pens and pencils, and extra copies of the school textbooks.

"What do you think?" She turned her anxious eyes towards her son. Wil felt a sudden flood of gratitude towards his mom.

"I think … he will love it."

"Really?"

"Yep, although he might not appreciate the textbooks."

Nora laughed and squeezed Wil's face between her hands. "Good. The hospital is most likely going to release him on Sunday. I've been trying to get everything ready." She moved over to the dresser and opened a couple of the drawers. "I hope I got his right size. I kept the receipts just in case. You boys grow out of your socks overnight."

"Mom, it's gonna be great." When she stopped fussing and smiled, he asked the question that had been bugging him. "How did you get it so that he could stay with us?"

"Oh, I got a petition for temporary custody. Officer Monroe put me in contact with someone at Social Services who helped me get the paperwork started. I've petitioned the courts to become his legal guardian ... if that's okay."

Wil stared at his mom. "You would do that?"

"Who else is going to take him? Some house full of strangers?" She shook her head as if that option could never be considered even while her cheeks flushed with shame. "I should have been paying closer attention and then maybe this wouldn't have happened."

Wil shook his head in protest, but she continued before he could speak.

"Scott has been a part of this family for as long as I can remember. It's only right that he live with us now."

"I know what you mean." A guilty look crossed Wil's face for just a second. He shook it off. "But I really think he's going to be okay. He's got a positive outlook."

"Maybe." She was silent for a moment. "So you don't think he'll mind?"

"No, he won't mind."

"And do you?"

Wil shook his head. "It might be kinda nice to have somebody else around."

A funny look flitted across her face. "My thoughts exactly." She moved towards the door. "It's been a little too quiet around here the last couple of years." Mother and son gazed at one another for a few seconds. She took his hand. "Come on. Let's go eat."

They started down the stairs. A thought occurred to Wil.

"Mom, are *you* gonna be okay to do this? I mean, can you afford to take in Scott? He eats a *lot*."

She chuckled. "Well, there is that, isn't there? I guess the raise from my new position should come in handy then, shouldn't it?"

Wil stopped in the kitchen doorway. "You got the job?"

"I did." She beamed at him. "Sam called yesterday to tell me the good news. You were a little preoccupied with Scott and everything. I didn't want to add any more to the emotional roller coaster."

"That's great, mom!" Wil hugged her and sat down. He spooned some lasagna onto her plate and then his. "You deserve it, more than anybody."

"Thank you, honey." A pensive look settled in her eyes, but she shook it off when Wil looked at her.

"What's the matter, Mom? Aren't you happy?"

"Very much so." Her voice didn't exactly match her words. "Now eat."

He didn't need much encouragement; he was nearly starving. For the first time in over a week, Wil felt the stirrings of happiness settling back over him. There was only one piece of the puzzle still missing, one piece that would have made him feel the world had righted itself out completely.

Chapter 10

Saturday morning dawned. Wil rolled over and rubbed his eyes. Morning sunlight sprayed in through the open window. Blue sky peeked at him through the leaves of the oak tree, blue with just a touch of white...

Wil bolted up and fled downstairs. Wrenching open the front door, he stepped onto the front porch, his eyes searching skyward. A thin line of clouds drifted in the distance, moving east, moving away from him.

Disappointment washed over him as he watched the white disappear in the vast blue. As he turned to go back inside, a familiar scent tickled at his nose, sweet and cinnamon-y.

Wil raced down the hallway and skidded to a stop in the kitchen doorway. His mom looked up in surprise.

"Good morning, honey. I didn't figure you would be that hungry after you ate all that lasagna last night. Guess I'm glad I made as many as I did."

She handed him a plate of French toast and turned to stir the cinnamon apples in the skillet.

A second wave of disappointment hit him, and he sat with sagging shoulders. His mom brought him some orange juice.

"You okay?" she asked with concern.

Wil toyed with the corner of a piece of toast. "Yeah. I'm fine."

She placed her hand under his chin and turned his face towards her. "Truth?"

Wil forced a smile he didn't feel. "Truth." She let go of him. "I was just sort of hoping ... there would be bacon."

She smiled. "Is that all?" Crossing to the stove, she picked up a plate of thick bacon strips. She set it down in front of him.

"Oh. Thanks." Wil made himself reach for a piece so she wouldn't worry.

"Whew! It looks like it's going to be another hot one today," his mom said as she sat across from him. "It would be nice if we could get a little cloud cover, block out that sun a little bit."

Wil didn't respond. He felt his mom looking at him. Biting off a piece of bacon so he wouldn't have to talk, he glanced up at her serious, worried expression.

"What?"

"Honey," she pushed her plate aside and clasped her hands together on the table, "I have something to ask you."

The cold stone began to settle in his stomach again. This time, however, Wil kept his face neutral.

"It's kind of bad timing, what with Scott and all, but since he's going to be okay, I was wondering if—"she took a deep breath, "you would like to meet Larry."

Wil glanced down at his breakfast. The cold stone grew a little bigger, but he ignored it. What was it Scott had said? *She's a nice lady, and she deserves to have someone take her out every once in a while.*

He returned his eyes to her face; she seemed so hopeful, so worried. He thought about the room upstairs waiting for Scott and her willingness to take on the burden of raising another teen-age boy. He thought about her sorrow on the day his dad passed away, her strength, her courage, her grief.

And he knew if he said no, she would let it go. She would stay unattached, unavailable for his selfishness.

"Okay." His voice sounded a tad unsteady, so he tried again. "Okay. I'll meet him."

The light on his mother's face washed away some of the doubt he felt. She struggled to keep her enthusiasm to a minimum.

"Great! I was thinking of inviting him over tonight, before we have to bring Scott home. Is that too soon?" Her anxiousness made him uneasy. "Maybe tomorrow would be better?"

Wil toyed with his bacon strip. He inhaled to keep his voice neutral. "Tonight's fine."

Mrs. Johnson clasped her folded hands under her chin and grinned at her son. Reaching over, she squeezed his hand.

"You'll see, Wil. He's a nice guy. You might end up liking him."

He nodded quietly and stood. "I think I'll go shower."

"Aren't you going to eat your breakfast? Aren't you hungry?"

He shook his head. "I'll save it for tonight's dinner." Then he smiled with as much enthusiasm as he could muster and left the room.

A NERVOUS ENERGY SETTLED ON Wil that afternoon. He had spent three hours at the hospital with Scott, watching with some amusement as Scott celebrated the lasagna and garlic bread. Wil had kept the conversation light, not mentioning the impending dinner or Scott's homecoming. He wanted to save that one as a surprise when his mom was around.

Janet had stopped by with a "Get Well Soon" balloon. Wil appreciated the interruption; he stood by the window, staring out at the bright blueness while Janet and Scott visited. He heard Janet mention something about thunder off in the distance, but as far as he could tell, the day was sunny, perfect, and cloudless. The brightness depressed him.

After leaving the hospital, Wil had come home to tend to his chores. He loaded the dishwasher and took out the garbage. Standing outside, he listened for the thunder Janet spoke of, but he didn't hear anything. The azure sky above pressed in on him.

"Oh, Cassia," he sighed, searching for any trace of wispy cloud. "Come back."

Nothing but a catbird answered him. He replaced the lid on the trashcan and went back inside.

His mother seemed to grow more and more nervous as the clock's hands ticked closer to seven o'clock. She quietly fussed over the table's settings, poked at the pork loin in the crock pot until Wil was sure all the moisture had escaped and left the meat dry and brittle, and wiped down the already clean counter three times.

When she began tugging at her skirt and smoothing out non-wrinkles in her blouse, Wil realized just how important this dinner was to her. He watched as she worried over an invisible flaw in her hair.

"Mom," he spoke up, startling her. "You look great. Everything looks great. Don't worry."

She smiled appreciatively at him and made a pretense of relaxing.

"You're right. How are you holding up?"

He shrugged. "I'm fine," he lied.

Just then the doorbell rang. Mrs. Johnson checked her reflection in the mirror one more time and smiled at her son.

"Ready?"

He nodded and moved to stand by the kitchen table. His mom hurried to answer the door, and he could hear two pleasant voices greet each other.

The cold stone tossed around inside his belly. He took a deep breath to steady it. *You can do this*, he thought. *She needs tonight.*

He turned to greet the man coming into the kitchen. His neutral expression changed to one of surprise, for in front of him was a familiar face. True, he wasn't in a uniform this time, but the sandy blond hair and green eyes on the handsome face was all too recognizable.

"Aren't you … the fireman who …?" Wil puzzled, his voice trailing off.

A friendly, pleasant smile crossed the man's face. Mrs. Johnson stepped between the two.

"Wil, honey, I'd like for you to meet Larry LaSalle. Larry, this is my son, Wil Johnson." She took Wil's arm affectionately as she introduced them.

"Hello, Wil. It's good to finally meet you." His voice sounded quiet but powerful. Wil took his outstretched hand and shook it, still wondering over the coincidence of it all.

"You came here the night of the fire." Wil struggled to grasp the situation. He looked at his mom. "You knew him then?"

She smiled apologetically. "It wasn't the right time for intro-ductions." A worried look creased her attractive face.

Wil turned his attention back to the man in front of him. He didn't want to ruin tonight for his mom. Neither, apparently, did Larry.

"You know, your friend was pretty lucky," he replied. "Your mom tells me he's going to be okay."

"Yeah, he is." Wil was grateful for the conversation. "It's a good thing you guys found him."

"Yes, it is." A funny look crossed Larry's face as the oven timer beeped. Mrs. Johnson left their sides and removed the biscuits from the oven.

"You know, it's kind of a strange situation," Larry continued. "You're probably going to think I'm crazy, what with this being our first meeting and everything, but, well, I told your mom, and she says it was just a fireman's intuition, but I think it was something else. It's almost like I heard this little voice inside my head saying, 'He's up there. He's in danger.' I know the fire chief thought I was off my rocker. Good thing he and I go way back together." Larry chuckled to himself and shook his head in bewilderment.

Wil stared at him. "You heard a voice?" It wasn't a question exactly.

Larry chuckled again, this time self-consciously. "Yeah. Sounds weird, doesn't it? Boy, some first impression, huh?"

"No," Wil replied after a moment. "I don't think it's weird at all. I'm glad you heard that voice. I know Scott's glad, too."

The two stared at each other, an awkward quiet descending upon them. Mrs. Johnson interrupted it.

"Okay, fellas, I do believe dinner is ready."

Wil took his seat thankfully.

"Boy, it sure smells good," Larry praised as he held out the chair for Nora. "Tell me, Wil, is your mom as good a cook as it appears?"

Wil smiled at his mom. "She's the best."

Mrs. Johnson returned his smile, though he could see the nervousness still etched in her eyes. He helped himself to the mashed potatoes and passed the bowl to Larry.

"So, how long have you been a fireman?" Wil tried again.

"Oh, let's see now—oh, thank you." Larry took a biscuit from the basket Wil held out to him. "I graduated from the academy in 1990, so that would make, what, eighteen years?"

"Do you like it?"

"There's nothing I'd rather be doing."

Wil felt the sincerity behind the words. He sliced open his biscuit and added some of the pork to it. "What's your favorite part about it?"

Larry grinned. "Playing hero, of course." He had a swallow of tea and nodded in approval. "Good tea. No, I think the best part is actually working in the community with the community, you know? There are a lot of really good people out there with good ideas, it's just they don't always know how or where to get started. I like being there when the positives happen, like the new youth center that's being built downtown."

"I hadn't heard about that," Mrs. Johnson spoke up.

"Mmmm, yeah. The plans have been approved, and they plan to break ground in two weeks. Oh, that reminds me, I need to call Joe about the baseball schedule."

"You play baseball?" Wil perked up.

"Sure do. The department has a league."

"Who do you play?"

"Other stations. Let's see, Macon, Ellington, Jasper, North Woods. We also have the annual Policemen/Firefighter's tournament. Calvin's cop house has held the trophy for the last five years. It must be all that chasing bad guys in the streets."

Wil smiled. The night wasn't turning out so bad after all.

"What position do you play?" He took a bite of mashed potatoes.

"Third base. You?"

"Pitcher."

"Yeah?"

"My dad taught me how to throw all the pitches when I was little. He *loved* baseball."

Nora stopped eating, her fork halfway to her mouth. She stared at her son. Wil looked down at his plate, stunned. He had mentioned his dad to a total stranger, and it had felt *good* to do so.

Larry glanced from mother to son and cleared his throat. "Pitching's tough," he continued as though there had been no pause. "You've got to have a good team behind you, and whoever's behind the plate most definitely needs to be on your side."

Wil shook himself from the sensation. "Yeah, well, it's usually Scott behind the plate. He's not much with a textbook and a calculator, but there's no one I'd rather have calling the shots."

He grew thoughtfully silent for a few minutes. As he chewed on his biscuit, he couldn't help notice the way his mom glanced at Larry. She seemed young and pretty and shy and sweet; the worry lines around her eyes had relaxed, and she had done very little to interrupt the conversation. Larry for his part seemed to respect the silence that had settled over the table. Wil liked the fact that Larry didn't appear to be one to keep conversation going for the sake of having a conversation. Companionable silence, that's what this felt like. No pretense, no forced politeness. Wil began to feel more comfortable with the idea of his mom and this man as friends. He wasn't ready to see it as anything more just yet.

When everyone had laid their forks down and sighs of contentment filled the air around the table, Nora stood up.

"I hope you have room for dessert, Larry. I made peach pie. There's coffee, too."

"Peach pie?" Larry looked at Wil, who nodded eagerly. His mouth watered at the thought, though his stomach groaned in protest.

"It's the best one she makes."

"I don't know about that." Larry pointed at the leftover food on the table. "It would have to be top of the line to beat this dinner. I'm used to station house meals, and I can tell you right now, Nora, you beat the captain's cooking by a mile."

She smiled and blushed a little at the compliment as she busily sliced the pie into six equal shares.

"Truly," Larry continued to Wil conversationally, "that man can coordinate a rescue out of a twelve-story burning building, but he can't toast bread. I'm telling you, the guys are gonna be so jealous when I return five pounds heavier."

Wil chuckled and took the plate his mom handed him. He spooned some Cool Whip onto his pie and watched as Larry took a bite.

"This is delicious," he said after a moment. "*This* is what the eating experience should be about."

"I'm glad you like it," Nora smiled. "Please have all you want."

He shook his head as he took another bite. "We have fire drills in the morning. I've already lost thirty seconds of speed, at least, with this meal."

Wil shared a glance of humor with his mom and raised his fork to his mouth. The cinnamon in the filling tickled his nose and made him wistful. He forced the bite to keep from thinking.

"Say, Wil, if you'd like, I could send you and your mom our game schedule once it's finalized, and you guys are welcome to come watch."

Wil thought about it for a second. "Yeah, that would be cool." Again, the cinnamon tickled his nose. "Wow, Mom, you must have added a lot more cinnamon this time. That's all I can smell."

Nora lifted a forkful to her nose and sniffed. "Mmm, no more so than usual, I don't think. I don't use a measuring cup," she added for Larry's sake. "I just measure by feel."

"Impressive." Larry smiled a charming smile at her.

Wil took another bite of the pie; the cinnamon scent filled his nostrils and gave him what he was sure was a cinnamon high. The sweet peaches dulled on his taste buds as the fragrance of apples mingled with the cinnamon.

He glanced up suddenly, his eyes wide.

"Honey, what is it?" Nora asked, alarmed at his expression.

Wil worked to relax his features. "Nothing. I just, um, I just remembered I have a project that's due on Monday for history. I should probably get started on it tonight."

Nora glanced at Larry, and Wil could see the concern settling on her face. "Do you have to do it right now?"

"It's a big project, Mom," he explained, the apology in his voice. "I kind of got behind because of, well, you know." Again, the cinnamon apple fragrance tickled his nose. He had to force himself to remain patient.

"Hey, it's okay with me," Larry interjected pleasantly. "I admire a guy that takes his studies seriously."

Nora looked at him, unsure. When she looked at Wil, he could see she wasn't entirely approving of this sudden interruption. He turned to Larry, attempting to find a graceful way to exit.

"It was, um, great meeting you, Larry." The sincerity behind the words surprised him a little.

"The pleasure, Wil, was all mine."

Wil stood a little awkwardly and picked up the remainder of his pie. "I'm just gonna, um, take this upstairs. Great dinner, Mom."

She smiled at him, and he could see her face had relaxed again. Wil forced himself to walk down the hall to the foot of the steps. The fragrance was stronger, calling to him, beckoning him upstairs.

He took the stairs two at a time and swung open his bedroom door. His room was empty; he set the uneaten peach pie down on his computer desk and hurried to the open window. Peering out, he spotted several clouds dotting the twilit sky.

Frowning, he withdrew his head and turned around. And there she was, lovely in the light radiating from her body.

"Cassia!" he exclaimed, crossing the room in three steps. Relief and joy settled over him as he stopped just short of stepping on her feet. He stared at her, his eyes taking in the brilliance of her white gown, the flawlessness of her hair twisted in the white cord, the fairness of her skin, and finally, the splendor of her crystal blue eyes.

"Where have you been?"

She smiled gloriously at him, her eyes crinkled in amusement. "I have been ... mending. A human shell is not easily repaired once it is cracked."

Wil immediately looked chagrined. "I'm so sorry about that. I don't know what happened that night. I didn't know you would ... that I could ... that it wasn't ..."

"Wil," she interrupted. "It is okay. I know it was not malicious on your part. If it had been, I would not be here now."

"So, then, you're not ... *angry* with me?"

Her face never lost its calm, somewhat amused expression. "I cannot feel anger, Wil, but even if I could, I would not be angry with you. What happened was not in your control. It was in no one's control, actually; it is just the way it is for us—what did you call us? *Cloud people?*"

Wil considered that. "What did happen, then?"

She folded her hands in front of her, hands that Wil had a sudden longing to touch, to feel her serenity again so that he could assure himself it really hadn't been his fault. He sat down on the bed instead and waited for her to speak.

"The blessings of Olin on his people are many, and they are

great. We are created with the ability to reason, to understand, to learn, and to adapt, traits that Olin recognized in the first humans who appeared on the earth. However, we are also limited in some ways; human emotions are a trait which we among the clouds do not possess. We know of love and truth and beauty and freedom, of acceptance and compassion, of gentleness and kindness. What we do not know of firsthand is the ability to feel hatred or anger or belligerence. We do not know what fury feels like, or disappointment, or the meanness that is sometimes illustrated by humans.

"One of the reasons we have studied humans for so long is that we wish to understand how these traits work. If we can learn the characteristics of these emotions and what triggers them and why they sometimes win out over love and decency, then it will bring our understanding of humans to a whole new level."

Wil nodded as he listened to her. "Okay, but I still don't understand why you went away? What made you … crack?" He grimaced at the last word, the image still all too clear in his mind.

"Those of my people who have been on this Earth for many moons have built up a resistance to such emotions, which makes their tasks as Gatherers much easier. Those of us new to Earth, new to firsthand experience with humans, like myself, have no such resistance. Our essences absorb every sensation emitting from humans. The impressions we are already familiar with do not phase us; they simply are integrated into our beings. However, the impressions with which we are not familiar do not get absorbed into our beings. Because we do not understand those feelings, it becomes difficult to process them, especially when they come so quickly at us."

"And you had just come from Scott's," Wil whispered as though to himself. "You were feeling all of those emotions that you didn't understand. What was that like for you?"

She paused and her look of calm was replaced for a moment with seriousness. "It was … difficult. What happened in that shelter produced a myriad of sensations with which I did not understand and could not integrate into my being."

"And then you came here and I—" Wil stopped. Shame overwhelmed him. He stood up and reached for her hands. At the last moment, he remembered himself and let his hands drop by his sides. "I don't know what to say. I am so sorry, Cassia. I just … lost it for a little while. I never meant to hurt you."

Her gentle smile caught him off guard. "I know that, Wil. You do not need to feel so concerned for me. You have actually done me a great service."

"How? I was mean to you! I blamed you for what happened to Scott—"

"Yes, and now that I have experienced some of these sensations firsthand, I am stronger. I have some resistance to these emotions now, so that should I ever be confronted with them again, I will be able to process them more easily."

Wil stared at her. "I don't believe this. You're supposed to be angry with me. You're supposed to say that you're leaving and never coming back because I'm such a jerk. You are *not* supposed to *thank* me for being a jerk."

It was her turn to stare at him. "I do not know what a jerk is, and I cannot feel anger, remember? Besides, this is what a Secret Keeper and a Gatherer do; they share information and experiences. It is never about right and wrong."

Wil rubbed his eyes with the bottoms of his wrists. "I don't know."

"Wil." She reached up and took his hands. Harmony and joy flowed gently across his soul, and he felt captured by the blue in her eyes. "Do not punish yourself. I would have returned sooner if I could have. I know how you have suffered as the days and nights have passed, but you do not need to dwell on it any longer. If you would like, we can call it a learning experience for both of us. Besides, Samson is convinced that had it not been for the fire at Scott's shelter, I might very well have been able to maintain my human form."

"I don't understand," Wil murmured. "What does the fire have to do with what happened to you?"

"Remember, fire is our enemy. It is the weapon of Meslo, the source of his power. As such, where it gives him his strength, it weakens my people considerably. It drains us of our abilities, our powers. Couple that with an overabundance of unfamiliar human emotions and..." She shrugged and squeezed his hands. Peace and tranquility rolled through him, a pleasant wave of emotions. He waited for it to settle before he trusted himself to speak.

"So, then, you're back? You're really back? To stay?"

"Yes. And now it is time for *you* to go."

Wil stared at her, perplexed. Her words didn't seem directed at him but at his window. He turned and flinched as if he had been hit; the blood drained from his face. On the windowsill perched the banshee, her pale green face contorted with ugly rage. Her lips were pulled back over the fangs, and she hissed and shrieked in fury. Long red fingernails, sharp and glistening with what looked like blood, gripped the window frame. Wil thought it looked like the banshee was either holding on for dear life or getting ready to pounce.

Cassia remained calm beside him. Releasing his hands, she took a step forward. "You cannot win here."

The banshee shrieked, a very poor sport. Her clawed hand slashed at Cassia and touched nothing but misty air.

"His soul is not for your taking." Cassia held out her hand, and a glowing orb appeared. "He passed the test."

With that, she hurled the orb at that banshee, who leapt, snarling, from the sill. Her red nails and bared fangs lunged for Wil. The orb slammed into her, obliterating her green body into dust. Cassia blew gently, and the dust sailed out of the window, disappearing into the deepening twilight.

Wil stared at Cassia. His legs felt weak and his throat dry. "The banshee," he croaked before sitting on the edge of his bed.

"Yes." He marveled at the calmness in Cassia's voice. "She has been residing here for quite some time."

Wil's eyes, the size of saucers, darted around his room. "What? Why?"

"To collect your innocence."

His startled look settled back on her patient face. She continued without waiting for his questions.

"There are many ways humans lose their innocence, Wil. Some lose it by giving up their belief in things they cannot see. Others lose it through betrayal or anger or acts of violence.

"When you began to lose yourself to your anger, she returned. She has been waiting for you to turn your back on what is important to you. It happens, even to the best of Secret Keepers. But do not worry. Your faith, your good heart, kept that from happening. She cannot touch you."

Her gentle smile melted some of the frozen fear Wil felt. He shook himself out of his stupor and asked thickly,

"If you could defeat her, why did you wait so long? She could have…" He couldn't finish the thought.

"I cannot make those choices for you, Wil. Humans have the ability to think and to reason, and once they have made up their minds, they must follow through, regardless of the consequences.

"However," and she smiled again, "I am your Guardian, and once you chose decency over malice, I was free to act."

Wil nodded and glanced around his room again. Seeing nothing but his own personal stuff did little to ease his worry.

She took his hand again, and comfort flowed through him. "Do not worry, Wil. You are safe, by your own choosing."

Wil smiled then. From outside the open window, quiet voices drifted up. Reluctantly, he pulled his hand away from Cassia; promptly, the comforting serenity left him. He stepped over to the window, cautious lest another banshee pounce at him, and peered out. Below, on the front porch, Larry and his mother stood talking.

Wil felt Cassia drift near, and he scooted over to make room for her. They watched together, silent witnesses to the pleasant conversation below.

"You know? I was sort of dreading tonight," Wil confessed,

finding a calming effect in talking. "And now I don't know why. Larry seems like a decent guy. My mom sure likes him."

"And you are conflicted. Why?"

A few lightning bugs danced outside the window. Wil watched them for a moment before answering.

"It's hard, seeing my mom with some other guy. I want her to be happy, but I don't want her to forget about my dad. I know this isn't fair, but I don't want anyone to replace my dad."

Cassia nodded as she scooped a handful of the dancing bugs into her hand. Little lights twinkled in the gradual darkness. Wil smiled to himself.

"Samson has explained the familial structure to me. That is his special interest among humans. It is rather fascinating the way you bond to certain people. We do not have any such structure in the clouds. We do have Prelectors, those who guide the young, such as myself, through our studies of the people of this world. However, we are … bonded to all the others from the moment we are formed. We have no resistance to any other being like ourselves."

She released the lightning bugs from her hand. They drifted away on the still night air.

"That's a lot of bonding," Wil commented with a grin. Even in the darkness of the infant night, he could see her clearly; her skin seemed to radiate a light as soft and mysterious as the moon.

She merely smiled at him and turned her attention towards the couple on the front stoop.

"I am curious, Wil. According to Samson, the familial bond is rather strong among humans, and from you, I sense an exceptionally strong attachment to the one you call 'dad.' I wonder why you should think anyone could replace him, if he is so imprinted on your soul the way he is."

He stared at her. "I guess it's hard to explain," he mumbled.

"You cannot forget someone who has made that strong of an impression on your essence. The same is true for your mom. One of the impressions Samson has gathered over his many moons of studies of humans is that you have an enormous capacity to love more than one person in more than one way. Do you agree?"

Wil continued to stare at her. He knew her words made sense; he just wasn't sure he could embrace them yet.

"I do agree," he admitted reluctantly. "But it doesn't happen very fast. Most times it takes...a long time before we can accept someone else."

"So you believe that you will be able to accept this Larry as a new person in your mom's life?"

"Maybe," he sighed, then grinned wickedly. "In a few moons."

Cassia smiled gloriously at him. A knock at the door drew his attention.

"Wil? Can I come in?"

Wil glanced back out the window. Larry was gone, his mother outside his door. He hadn't even noticed their parting. He hadn't noticed Cassia's parting, either. Empty space now sat beside him. He looked around, bewildered.

"Wil?"

"Yeah, Mom. Come on in."

She pushed open the door and stepped in, her eyes cautiously searching for him in the darkness. Instinctively, she flipped on the overhead light. Wil blinked in the sudden brightness.

"You okay, honey?" she asked.

"Yeah." He pointed at the open window behind him. "Just letting in some fresh air. I didn't hear Larry leave."

"Yeah. He's got that training tomorrow." She paused. "I just wanted to thank you for tonight, Wil. I know it wasn't easy for you, but you did great, and that means so much to me."

"It's okay, Mom." Wil shrugged it off, somewhat embarrassed. "It actually turned out better than I expected. Larry seems...okay. You were right. I think I like him."

Nora's face relaxed, and she suddenly looked ten years younger. "Oh, honey, I'm so glad! He really liked you. That's all he talked about outside, what a good kid you were. Well, you know me. I simply couldn't argue with his opinion."

Wil grinned self-consciously. "Yeah, well, I don't know how well I'll do at it, Mom, but I promise you, I'm gonna try."

"That's all I ask, sweetheart." She touched his cheek gently with the back of her hand. "And you don't have to worry. We're going to take it slow, not just for you, although ... you are a big reason. But truthfully? I'm a little rusty at the dating game. So is he."

Wil chuckled. "Well, you both looked like pros to me."

She smiled and glanced at the picture of the family at the Grand Canyon. Her finger touched her husband's smiling face for a brief second. "Yeah." When she looked back at Wil, he noticed a trace of sorrowful wistfulness on her face; it didn't last long.

"Goodnight, sweetheart. We're picking Scott up around two o'clock tomorrow."

"Okay. 'Night, Mom."

As soon as she had shut his door, the scent of cinnamon apples drifted in through the window. He turned to see Cassia hovering just outside his window, her legs crossed in a sitting position.

"That was difficult for you," she observed, "but it made her very happy."

"Yeah, well, my mom's a good person. Scott was right about that. She does deserve to be happy."

Wil gazed at her for a moment. She smiled at him.

"Do what you need to do, Wil. The banshees are gone."

He shook off the last of his nervousness. "I don't know if you realize it or not, Cassia, but you're not exactly the easiest person to ignore."

She considered for a moment, then grinned knowingly at him. With a wave of her hand, she transformed into the wispy mist and lingered near the leaves of the tree.

"Very cool." Wil chuckled to himself before turning towards his bed.

Chapter 11

Scott's voice carried through the open door and down the hospital corridor. Wil quickened his step.

"I told you I'm not going to any foster home," Scott argued with the social worker standing patiently in the doorway.

"You don't really have a choice," she responded calmly as Wil walked in. "The law clearly states that you are still a minor. You must be placed in a supervisory atmosphere. It's either this home or the group home."

Scott scowled at her, his green eyes dark and stormy.

"Dude," Wil said in an attempt to lighten the mood, "stop giving the lady a hard time."

"I already told you, I'm not going," Scott insisted stubbornly. "I don't want to live with a bunch of do-gooders."

The social worker shifted her stance, her mouth pursed against a smile. Wil shrugged helplessly.

"Well, from what I've heard, they're not so bad. I mean, there's even a kid your age, so at least you'll have someone to hang around with."

"I don't want to 'hang around with' some loser because the state tells me I have to. And where do they live, huh? Probably on the other side of town. That's the other school district, Wil; I'll end up catching against you and having to baby-sit some no-talent joker on the mound. That's not gonna happen. Can't your mom do something?"

"She's done everything she can," Wil replied apologetically. "The state says it has to be this way, but don't worry. We'll still hang out."

"When? On the weekends? Every other Wednesday? No way." Scott turned his dark eyes on the social worker again. "This is not my fault. I didn't burn down the house. I didn't almost kill myself. Why am I being punished?"

"It's not a punishment, Scott," the social worker replied. "It's what's in your best interest."

"Oh, yeah. Living with a bunch of strangers miles away from my friends. I can see where that would be in my best interest."

"There is the group home here in town, if you would prefer."

Scott sulked quietly; Wil could see the frustration etched into his face, the corners of his mouth pulled down slightly at the idea of leaving what was familiar. He resisted the urge to grin and instead forced a compassionate expression.

Nora bustled into the room at that moment, her hand full of papers that she busily scanned with her eyes, her lips moving slightly over the words. She looked up and smiled.

"Hello, Scott. I'm so glad to see you out of that bed." She hugged him and ruffled his hair affectionately. "Well, now, you've been checked out of the hospital, so all that's left is for you to say good-bye—"

"I'm not doing this!" Scott cried suddenly, tears of frustration threatening to fall. "I swear to God, I'll run away before I live as a foster kid! Mrs. J., can't you do something, *anything*?"

"Didn't you tell him, Wil?"

Wil grinned sheepishly at his mom and shrugged his shoulders. "I hadn't gotten to that part yet." He looked at Scott. "My mom fixed it so you could stay with us. We're gonna be your do-gooder foster family. Surprise."

Scott blinked, the dark green of his eyes lightening to jade. A flush crept into his cheeks as he gazed at Nora. "I'm going home ... with you?"

"That was the plan, but if there's someplace else you'd rather—"

"No! No, that's great. That's perfect."

Nora smiled. "Good. Now unless you plan on getting on the payroll, I suggest we head on out of here." She turned towards the social worker. "Thank you, Delores, for setting this up."

"No problem. I will need to talk to you about a visitation schedule."

"Sure. I've got a pocket calendar in my glove compartment. We can look at that." Nora headed out of the room with Delores. Wil, amused, and Scott, chagrined, hung back.

"Loser, huh?" Wil feigned hurt.

"Yeah. That was a bit uncalled for," Scott replied, feigning remorse. "I should have said 'asshole.' You knew the whole time."

"I was just having too much fun watching you make a jerk of yourself."

"Yeah, well, I learned from the master, Punk." Scott grinned at him. "Your mom really likes me."

Wil sighed as the two headed for the exit. "Yeah, like a good plague. I tried to talk her out of it, but she insisted with her 'Jerks need love, too' philosophy."

"Thank god for the humanity in that woman."

They stopped at the car where Nora was penciling in information on her calendar. Scott shifted before Delores.

"Look, um, I'm sorry about giving you a hard time in there. *Certain* people didn't tell me certain things," he shot Wil a pointed look, "and I, well, I'm sorry."

Delores chuckled. "Don't worry about it, Scott. I've dealt with tougher. Good luck. Here's my card if you ever need to reach me. Good-bye, Nora. Call me if you need anything."

"Good-bye, and thank you." Nora slid into the driver's seat, and the boys climbed into the car. As she pulled out of the parking lot, Nora glanced at Scott sitting comfortably in the back seat.

"You know, Scott, I don't know if they told you about your dad, but they found him … and they arrested him."

Wil glanced over his shoulder; Scott stared out the window, his expression impassive. Nora exchanged a look with her son and made a left turn. Her eyes darted back to the rearview mirror.

"He's still in jail. He didn't have the bail money. We could go by there, if you'd like."

"No. I'm okay."

Wil glanced over his shoulder again. Scott's voice betrayed no emotion, and his gaze didn't turn from the window.

"Okay." Nora kept her voice neutral as she spoke. "We'll go when you're ready."

Scott made no reply. The rest of the drive was quiet. Wil felt a great sense of relief when his mom pulled into their driveway. Scott followed him into the house and up the stairs.

"Mom fixed this room up for you," Wil said, breaking the silence, which was starting to make him a little nervous.

Scott nodded and pushed open the door. His eyes lit up with sudden surprise as he noticed the iPod, the shoes, and the baseball mitt.

"What's this?" he asked, stepping over to the bed. He picked up the mitt and stared at it.

Nora shrugged from the doorway. "I figured it'd be awfully hard for you to catch Wil's heaters bare-handed."

Scott gazed at her, stunned affection on his face. "Thanks, Mrs. J. This is … the nicest thing anybody's ever done for me."

She smiled. "There are clothes in the dresser drawers. Try some of them on and whatever doesn't fit, we can take back tomorrow." She glanced at Wil. "I'm going to go take care of some things downstairs. Call me if you need me."

She left the two boys alone in the room. Scott worked the mitt on his hand.

"Your mom is the best lady ever."

"Yeah, she is." Wil watched his friend for a moment. "You know, if you want to talk about your dad and what happened—"

"I don't." Scott tossed the mitt on the bed and picked up the book off the nightstand. He stared at the cover. "*Peter Pan*. I used to love this story."

"I know. I found it in my room, and I thought you might want to have it."

"I always wanted a little fairy, you know, to shake some dust on me so I could fly away. Neverland seemed like paradise, and after my dad, well, who could be afraid of Captain Hook?"

"Scott—"

"Thanks." He set the book back on the nightstand and picked up the iPod. "Mind if I use your computer to get some songs downloaded?"

"Sure." Wil stepped aside as Scott crossed the hallway.

"I was gonna run away."

Scott's sudden confession brought Wil up short. He stood in the doorway of his bedroom and stared at his friend. Scott fidgeted with the iPod; his expression mixed relief with matter-of-factness.

"I had a bus ticket," he continued, nodding to himself as though convincing himself it was all right to disclose this secret. "I wasn't entirely convinced I was going to use it, it just seemed ... necessary to have it, like a security blanket, you know? Anyway, my dad found it and flipped out. He didn't take too kindly to my wasting money on a bus ticket when there was good, hard liquor to buy."

Though he attempted to keep his voice light, the bitterness crept in anyway. Wil remembered that night (had it really only been two weeks?) and mentally kicked himself again. Scott looked up then and forced a grin.

"Anyway, I'm glad I didn't use that ticket. Besides," he added to cover the uncomfortable silence lingering between them, "you'd be totally lost without me."

"Totally," Wil agreed. Scott nodded and sat down at the computer. As he waited it for it to warm up, he glanced around the room.

"What is *this*?" he demanded, getting up again and crossing the room to stand in front of a poster. Wil stood beside him; the two boys gazed at the girl in cowboy boots and cut-off shorts. Her checkered blouse was tied around her waist. Two brown pig tails hung over her shoulders, and on her head sat a cowboy hat. She smiled at the two boys, her lips cherry red, her hands on her hips.

"I think her name is Becky," Wil answered. He shrugged at his friend. "It was on sale."

Scott laughed. "Much better. Much, *much* better than Harry Potter. I'm proud of you. My influence on you is proving positive after all."

Wil made a face and picked up a rolled-up poster where it leaned against the wall. "Here you go. Her name's Nancy or Nellie or something like that."

Scott unrolled the poster and sighed. "Oh, hel-lo, Nancy. I've missed you."

"Want to hang it up?"

"You bet. Right over the bed."

"Mmm, I don't think Mom will go for that."

Scott considered. "All right, the foot of the bed then. Something this beautiful should be seen as often as possible."

Wil shook his head. "Come on, Loverboy. I'll help you."

"Did I mention how glad I am to live here?"

"Yeah, yeah, yeah. Didn't you say something once about 'spouting sentimentality'?"

"Nauseating, isn't it?"

"A little."

Scott laughed and trotted across the hall. Wil shook his head and followed him. Outside the window, the clouds drifted lazily across the blue sky.

MONDAY PROVED TO BE AN interesting day. Talk of the end-of-the-year school dance was on everyone's lips. Scott found himself in the role of "cele-bri-tee"; Chris and Derek both clapped him on the back and said they were glad he was back because school had proven just too boring without him. Janet, Laurie, and even Stacey Jo hugged him the minute they saw him. Various members of the baseball team called out to him in the hallways, and his teachers made sure to note publicly his return at the beginning of each class. By lunch, Wil found the whole thing absurdly comical.

"I feel like you need a bodyguard," he teased as they walked into the cafeteria.

"No, no. A star must be willing to meet his public openly," Scott replied, casting a mock wave to the crowd.

"Is the rule the same for a moron?"

"Ah, see, now you wound me. I will have to fire you from the payroll."

"This is a paying job?"

"Not anymore."

The two of them sat down and began unpacking their lunch bags. Wil glanced around, looking for Cassia. She had been conspicuously absent that morning, though Wil was positive none of his teachers had noticed. He spotted a lone figure sitting at the table in the back corner of the cafeteria. After a moment's hesitation, he stood and made his way to the table. Andrew looked up as he approached.

"Hey," Wil said, shoving his hand into his pocket.

"Hey." A book lay in front of Andrew. Wil glanced at the title.

"So you finished the second one. What'd you think?"

"It was good. That part about Jacob was cool."

The two stared at each other. Wil shrugged off the awkwardness.

"Do you want to come sit with us?"

"What?"

"My friends." Wil glanced their way. "We have room."

Andrew scratched his head, considering. "Okay. Sure."

He picked up his book and followed Wil back to the table. The others stared at the two of them.

"Guys, this is Andrew," Wil said by way of introduction. "And that's Scott, Stacey Jo, Chris, Derek, Laurie, and Janet. He's gonna sit with us, if that's okay."

Scott glanced from Andrew to Wil, then at the rest of the table. No one else seemed sure of what to say, so it was Scott who nodded first.

"Yeah."

Wil grinned at him and slid his lunch down one seat. Andrew sat in between the two of them, right across from Laurie. The redhead smiled at Andrew and ducked her head shyly, her cheeks coloring slightly.

Derek glared at her and turned to Chris.

"Girls," he muttered.

"So, Scott," Chris asked, "are you going to be able to play in the game today?"

"Nope. I can practice, but that's about it."

"That sucks, too," Wil replied. "That means Allan's behind the plate."

"He's pretty good," Chris commented.

"Only when Mike's on the mound," Scott informed him. "That's the only one he'll try to talk through a game. I can't figure him out."

"Mike's a sophomore. So's Allan. Maybe it's freshmen bias," Janet suggested.

"That's stupid," Laurie replied. "Aren't they all on the same team?"

"Yep, but maybe Allan thinks Mike's a better pitcher," Chris added.

"Wil out-throws him."

Everyone looked at Andrew. He shook his shaggy brown hair out of his eyes in an effort to throw off the embarrassment he now felt.

"How do you know?" Derek asked.

Andrew shrugged. "I've kept track."

Scott made a face at Wil. "I knew it. A catcher has a feel for these things."

Wil shrugged modestly. "Well, that's not going to help us very much today. Mike starts today, and he was pretty sharp in practice on Friday."

"You guys coming?" Derek asked.

"I am. Gina's got Girl Scouts after school today, so I'm in the clear," Chris replied, throwing his trash onto his tray.

"I may be benched, so to speak, but I am definitely gonna be there," Scott said as the bell rang.

Wil looked at Andrew as they stood up. "What about you?"

"Haven't missed one yet. Oh, except for that time I was suspended."

"Why don't you come out for the team?" Wil asked as they headed for third period.

"What, you mean a stellar student like myself? I don't think so."

"There's always next year."

"We'll see. Say, have you seen Cassia lately?"

"Yeah, I saw her Saturday. You?"

"Yesterday. She tell you that stuff about the battles? It kinda blew my mind. And what are we supposed to do with all of this information anyway?"

"I don't know. I think we're just supposed to know it. I think that's what being a … Secret Keeper is all about."

"Anything like this ever happen to you before?" Andrew paused outside a classroom.

"Nope. You?"

"Not even close. See you in fourth?"

"I'll be there." Wil punched him in the arm and trotted off towards his class.

Well done, Wil Johnson.

He paused in front of the window overlooking the courtyard. A thin wisp of cloud hung low in the sky. Grinning, he waved and hurried into his class just as the tardy bell rang.

WIL LEANED HIS HEAD DESPAIRINGLY against the fence. The scoreboard flashed the score under the darkening sky: Home–2, Visitor–6, Inning–5.

Runners stood poised on first and second. Mike was behind in the count, and Wil's team only had one out. His coach stood by the opening to the dugout, watching as Mike threw a third ball.

"Johnson, get ready," his coach said after a moment. Wil shrugged out of his jacket and picked up his glove. "Time!"

The coach trotted out to the mound, conferred with Mike, then waved Wil out to the mound.

"Good effort, Mike," Wil said, smacking gloves with the former pitcher. He took his place on the mound and began throwing warm-ups. On the other side of the first base fence stood Scott, Andrew, and Chris, cheering him on. After several warm-ups had been thrown, the coach took the ball from Wil.

"All right, Johnson. We need these outs. They are pulling everything to left field. See what you can do about evening things out a little bit."

"Right, Coach." Wil took the ball handed him and tossed it to the umpire as his coach trotted off the field.

"All right, Wil!" Derek called out. "Let's go. Nothing but strikes, baby, right here. Here we go!"

Wil kicked at the mound and looked at the fence while setting his foot. Scott glanced at the batter, flashed a sign, and rubbed his eye as though he had dirt in it.

Wil grinned to himself and leaned over. He shook off each sign until Allan called the one he wanted. The pitch he threw sailed towards the plate and dropped at the last second.

"Strike!" called the umpire.

"Yeah!" cheered Scott, Chris, and Andrew as the umpire held up a fist.

Wil caught the ball, set himself, and waited for the sign. Going into his windup, he spot-checked the runners, then threw. The ball sailed towards the plate and dropped under the batter's swing.

Wil's team cheered as the batter trotted towards the dugout.

"One more, guys, one more!" Derek announced, holding up two fingers for everyone to see.

Wil watched the fence where Andrew and Scott were busy conferring with the book. Andrew said something, and Scott nodded in agreement. Wil set his foot; Scott flashed a sign, this time scratching his head afterwards.

Wil's first pitch crossed the plate off the inside corner. His second pitch seemed too fast for the batter, who swung a second too late and caught only a piece of it. The third pitch hit the inside corner again, much to the batter's dislike.

As Wil's team trotted to the dugout, Wil made a pit stop by the fence.

"Pretty sharp, Wil," Chris praised.

"Yeah, well, I'm only as good as my catcher."

"What's his deal?" Scott asked, cutting a look at the plate.

"He wants the heaters."

"Is he paying attention to the game? They've been tearing up the heaters all over the left side of the field," Andrew commented.

"That's why I pay *you* the big bucks," Wil replied pointedly to Scott. He waved at them and disappeared into the dugout as Scott asked, "This is a *paying* job?"

When Wil took to the mound a few minutes later, his team failing to score that inning, he caught a whiff of cinnamon. Andrew caught his eye and tilted his head sideways in a gesture. Looking around, Wil spotted Cassia sitting on top of the dugout, her legs crossed, a glorious smile on her face.

Wil held up his glove in greeting, then threw a few warm-ups. The game proceeded in the same fashion, with Wil getting Scott's call from the fence and setting up his pitch accordingly. Cassia watched each pitch with great interest, following the ball into the catcher's glove or into the air or onto the ground, wherever it happened to fall. From the fence, Scott, Chris, and Andrew busily discussed each play, pitch, and hit in between cheers. When all was said and done, Wil's team lost, six to two, but he didn't feel upset about it. Rather, he felt peaceful about the whole afternoon. That innocuous feeling intensified later that evening when Scott, seemingly buried under a pile of make-up work, surfaced long enough to comment, "You were right about Andrew, Wil. He's not such a bad guy. That book of his is incredible! Did you know he's got stats on every player from this season, including what their best pitches seem to be? It's like a baseball Bible."

"I told him he should see about playing next year," Wil replied, punching in some numbers on his calculator. "He doesn't think he can make it because of his grades."

"I'll have to talk to him," Scott mused. "Convince him to look past the struggle of grades. I mean, I've managed to keep a high enough average. I'll bet if I can do it, so can he. Our lives aren't really that different."

Wil looked at him across the top of the dining room table and grinned knowingly. When he returned his attention to his math a few seconds later, it was with a contented sigh.

"No, they aren't."

LATER THAT WEEK, THE NEXT to the last Friday in the school year, Wil and Scott made their way to Sally's Soda Shoppe. The two friends took their time and cut through the park; their voices sliced through the stillness of the air as they debated the talent of their baseball heroes: who had the best ERA, who had the meanest curveball, who was more likely to get a successful steal. Suddenly, Scott stopped and grabbed Wil by the arm, his grip vicelike.

"Ow!"

"Oh my god. That's her." Scott pointed, and Wil followed his friend's finger. Cassia sat on top of a picnic table, feeding pigeons from her hand.

Wil turned puzzled eyes to his friend. Scott's face flushed with excitement, although his voice whispered in surprise.

"That's my guardian angel. Cassia!" Scott gazed at Wil, his green eyes almost giddy with recognition.

Wil shook his head, unable to believe what he was hearing. "What do you mean, your 'guardian angel'?"

"It was her voice I heard that night telling me to get out." Scott turned his attention back to Cassia.

"How do you know?"

"Because I saw her," Scott answered in a rush. His declaration surprised him, and he blinked. "I did," he repeated almost to himself. "I saw her right before she ... vanished, like a hallucination."

Wil stared at him. "You saw her."

Scott grinned. "Yeah. My guardian angel." A new expression settled on his face: gratitude mixed with understanding and (Wil felt the cold stone settling in his stomach) honest admiration.

Scott left his side and trotted over to where Cassia sat, a butterfly resting on her finger. Wil followed reluctantly. She smiled gloriously at them.

"Greetings, Wil. Greetings, Scott."

"Hi, Cassia." Scott beamed at her, his cheeks flushed. Wil merely smiled at her; he couldn't deny the feeling in his stomach, a combination of sorrow for Scott and jealousy for himself, though what there was to be jealous about, he didn't know. He watched the butterfly flutter away.

"What are you doing in the park?" Scott asked.

"Oh, I always come here," Cassia answered. She eyed Wil curiously, and he knew she felt his trepidation. With a conscious effort, he pushed the feeling away. Cassia blinked in surprise, but her expression didn't change. "I like to feed the birds."

"Well, we're on our way to Sally's," Scott continued, taking

Cassia's hands and helping her off the table. Wil had the vague impression he had been completely forgotten. "Why don't you come with us?"

"What is Sally's?"

"It's a soda shop," Scott explained, and Wil couldn't help noticing he hadn't taken his eyes off of her face. "We're going to have ice cream."

"Ice cream?"

"Yeah. Sally makes the best. Sundaes, splits, milkshakes."

"What—?"

"It's a type of food," Wil answered her unspoken question. Scott shot him a look, as though he had suddenly remembered Wil was with him. "You'll like it."

Cassia studied him with her quiet blue eyes. Wil shifted and pretended nonchalance.

"Yeah. Come with us," Scott coaxed. "We're meeting Andrew. He's a … friend, I guess you could say."

"Andrew?" Cassia's eyes lit up. She smiled radiance. "Yes. I will come with you. I should like to experience this … milkshake for myself."

Scott beamed, and Wil would swear his friend had just won the lottery. He hung back a little and watched as Scott and Cassia walked ahead of him. Pieces of this puzzle seemed ragged and ill-fitting. Trying to figure out what had happened in the last three minutes was giving him a headache.

Cassia glanced over her shoulder at him and smiled.

Do not be troubled, Wil. I am pleased you are going to share this milkshake experience with me.

He blinked as her words filled his head. He met her look and felt some of his puzzlement melt away. Not as effective as if she had taken his hand, but pretty close.

Breathing to himself, he caught up with them as they rounded the corner. Sally's Soda Shoppe sat on the corner, its front windows and door bowed in the shape of the curb. Teenagers lounged outside the doors, reveling in the late spring warmth while slurping milkshakes, licking ice cream cones, or sharing banana splits.

Scott led the way inside; the bright red and yellow walls overwhelmed Cassia's eyes, and she blinked several times. In the corner booth, curved like a side-ways "C," sat Andrew. He waved at them, his face breaking into a huge smile as he noticed Cassia.

The friends slid into the booth, Cassia seated between Andrew and Scott. Wil sat across from her, grateful that now he could watch Scott and see if he really *did* see Cassia. So far, the only emotion Scott showed was newborn infatuation.

"Greetings, Andrew. It is good to see you again." Cassia regarded the changes in Andrew: his hair, though still thick and floppy, had been neatened by a recent cutting; his fingernails had been scrubbed clean, and he sported a new green tee shirt. She nodded to herself, pleased, and Wil knew there was something much deeper she saw that was the cause of her pleasure.

"You, too." He ducked his head shyly; then, as if remembering he was supposed to the tough guy, he leaned back casually and toyed with his napkin. "You sure do make the mutts at this table look a hell of a lot better."

"Here, here," Wil agreed.

"Speak for yourselves," Scott pouted. "I am quite comfortable in my mutt-i-ness. Not everybody can carry it off with my style."

Wil rolled his eyes.

"You should be comfortable with it," Andrew ragged. "You make the strays on Toplin Road look like pedigrees. Tell me, how hard is it for you to lick yourself?"

Scott, although a little flustered, didn't miss a beat. "Not as hard as it is for the mutt with nothing *to* lick."

"And that, my man," Andrew leaned around Cassia and slapped five with Scott, "is how you throw an insult."

Cassia, who had followed their conversation with perplexity, opened her mouth to ask a question. Wil caught her eye and shook his head dismissively. She took his advice and smiled up at the waitress who arrived at their table.

"Hi, kids. What'll it be?"

"A hot caramel sundae with extra whipped cream," Scott answered immediately. "I've had all day to think about it," he informed the others.

"And you, sweetie?" The waitress looked at Cassia.

"I do not—" she started, but Wil jumped in, saving her.

"Milkshake."

She glanced at him; he nodded and smiled at her.

"Peach," he continued, "and I'll have chocolate."

"'Kay, and for you?" The waitress jotted down the orders and looked at Andrew.

"Hot fudge sundae."

The waitress left to fill their orders.

"The last game is Monday," Andrew commented. "Are you going to play, Scott?"

"Yep. Coach told me today after practice. And Wil starts. Last game of the season, I guess he wants the best out there."

Wil shrugged modestly.

"You should come to the game, Cassia," Scott invited. "You'd like it."

"I like baseball very much," she smiled at him.

Scott seemed to melt under her smile. "Well, uh, you should, um, come watch Wil pitch. He's a great pitcher. Got a mean sinker."

"I do not know what a 'sinker' is, but I have seen him pitch. He is very good." She glanced at Wil, feeling that unfamiliar something that had been wrapping itself around his essence since the park. There was the conscious struggle to suppress the sensation; unfortunately, he wasn't very successful.

At that moment, the waitress returned and set the treats on the table. Cassia watched as Andrew rubbed his hands together.

"Oh, boy! I haven't had one of these in so long." He scooped up a generous spoonful and stuffed it into his mouth. Relish washed over his face, and he closed his eyes in dramatic appreciation.

"And this pleases you," Cassia observed, amused.

"Oh, it pleases me very much." Andrew grinned at her and took another bite.

"It's the whipped cream," Scott added. He spooned the fluffy white cream. "And the caramel and the vanilla ice cream and ooh! A cherry!" He popped it into his mouth and smiled at her.

"Try yours, Cassia," Wil said, stirring his milkshake and wishing Scott wouldn't look at her *that* way.

She met his eyes, and he could see she still puzzled over something she sensed from him. After a minute, she focused on the tall glass in front of her; a pale peachy color filled the glass to the rim and then was lost underneath the fluffy whiteness Scott had referred to as "whipped cream."

Although a straw stuck out of the glass, Cassia followed the leads of Scott and Andrew and picked up the long-handled spoon on the table. Slowly she scooped some of the ice cream onto her spoon and placed it in her mouth. The cold touched her tongue first, then the fruity flavor of peaches. Her human fingers tingled, and warmth spread all the way to her human toes.

Wil heard Andrew's spoon clatter to the table; looking at Cassia made his own stomach flip-flop, for a lovely brilliance, like that of the moon, surrounded her. Her cheeks flushed the color of apricots, and her eyes sparkled ocean blue. Suddenly, she faded into wispy cloud before popping back into her human form. The blip lasted for just a second, and she didn't even seem aware of it. Her smile glowed, and she exhaled with pleasure.

"Whoa." Andrew exchanged a startled look with Wil. Wil wasn't sure what Andrew was feeling, but his stomach hadn't stopped flip-flopping, and his pulse seemed to be in a race for life.

"First milkshake, huh?" drawled Scott, and Wil didn't have to wonder at *his* feelings. He stared at her, his cheek resting in his hand. "It does good for you."

Cassia's smile faded as she noticed his expression. She glanced at Wil, then Andrew, then Wil again. Their expressions were easier to read. Wil shook his head again, and his eyes darted to Scott. She understood and remained quiet.

Scott seemed to snap out of his reverie. He pushed his treat away from him, seeming a little disoriented.

"I don't... feel... very good," he said, dazed. "I'm gonna go... I'll be back in a minute."

Cassia watched him stumble off to the restroom.

"What has happened?" she asked when he was out of earshot.

Wil looked at Andrew, who shrugged helplessly.

"You, um, sort of, um, glowed," he tried to explain.

"More than usual," Andrew added. "Majorly."

"And," Wil continued, "you sort of... phased into cloud. For just a second," he added in a rush as she glanced, startled, at her human hands.

"It was pretty awesome," Andrew said with a grin.

Cassia relaxed after a moment. "I do not know why that happened, but at least no one else could see me. I will ask Samson when next I... what is it?"

Wil stared at her, concern on her face. "The thing is," he stammered, "I don't know if... if Scott saw you."

"What do you mean?" Andrew demanded. "He can't see her, can he?"

"I don't know. He said he saw you the night of the fire, right before you vanished."

"That cannot be." Cassia considered this new bit of information. "I do not... no, I do not sense him that way. He is not a Secret Keeper."

"Well, he saw *something* just now," Andrew stated.

Cassia slid from the booth. "I must go. If he did see something, Rayle needs to know so he can erase it from Scott's mind." She stood silent for a moment. "Something does not feel right." She looked at them and made the familiar gesture. "Until we meet again."

With that, she sailed out the door, her cloud form taking over before she had hit the sidewalk.

Scott returned to the table a minute later. His color looked normal, though his eyes still held a stunned look.

"Where's Cassia?" he asked as he sat back down.

"She, um, had to get home for dinner," Wil lied. "Are you okay? I've never seen you turn down food before."

"I don't know what happened," Scott confessed. "When she ate that milkshake ... it was like she glowed."

Andrew and Wil exchanged looks with one another.

"What do you mean?" Andrew asked, leaning forward.

Scott stared at him. "Surely you guys saw it. I mean, she was the most beautiful girl I've ever seen. Don't you think so?"

"Yeah," Andrew answered, perplexed.

"I didn't know ice cream could do that to a person." Scott seemed to consider something. "I think I'm going to ask her to the dance. You think she'd go with me?"

Wil worked harder to keep his face neutral than he ever had before in his life. The cold stab in his stomach didn't seem to mix too well with his chocolate milkshake.

"I don't know." His voice sounded very far away. "I don't know if she's even planning on going."

He noticed Andrew watching the conversation between them with fascination. Wil instinctively knew the questions on the tip of Andrew's tongue, and he knew he didn't want to know the answers to any of them.

At that moment, Scott brushed his hand by his cheek, once, twice. He looked around as if expecting to see a spider's web, then blinked widely. A dazed look came over him again for the briefest of seconds. His expression grew confused.

"Why are we just sitting here?" he asked. "Why is our ice cream going to waste? Why are there four glasses?" The last question bewildered him the most.

"You don't remember?" Andrew asked in wonderment.

"No." Scott thought for a moment. "Somebody was with us, weren't they?"

"Yeah. It was Chris," Wil answered quickly.

"Where'd he go?"

"He got called home while you were in the bathroom."

"You guys want to go to a movie?" Andrew asked, attempting to change the subject.

"Yeah," Wil agreed readily. "Isn't that new Batman movie playing?"

"That one is supposed to be really cool," Andrew played along.

"Come on, Scott. We can call mom from the cinema. She won't care, not on a Friday night." Wil slid out of the booth, eager to play the charade for as long as necessary. "What about you, Andrew? Will the home care?"

"Nah. I'll just check in with my guardian. As long as I'm back by nine-thirty and he knows where I am, it's cool."

Scott still sat, puzzled. "Are you sure it was Chris?" he asked them. "I would swear it was..." He tapped the side of his head, visibly straining to remember.

Andrew shot a look of desperation at Wil.

"Hey, Scott, I hear that Nina Selna might be at the movies tonight. Stacey Jo was talking about a group of them going to see *Batman*."

"Nina Selna?" Scott's confusion faded. "Then why are we still sitting here? Come, gentlemen, let us to the cheerleaders!"

Wil breathed a sigh of relief. He and Andrew followed him out of Sally's into the late afternoon sun setting in the west.

Chapter 12

The school year rolled to an end. Although Wil stayed busy enough, he still had a few moments each day to notice Cassia's absence. He didn't know whether the incident at Sally's Soda Shoppe had prevented her return, or if her absence was by her own choosing. What he did know was that Scott seemed to be over his infatuation, so he was sure that whatever Rayle had done had been successful.

In fact, Scott seemed to be going out on a rather high note. He and Wil led their baseball team to a victorious last game, with Wil pitching a no-hitter and Scott driving in a three-run homer late in the sixth inning. Nora had taken the boys to a steakhouse to celebrate and, at Wil's request, Larry had joined them. Scott took to Larry right away, reveling in his daring tales of fierce fires and bold rescues. Larry, for his part, did not mention Scott's rescue or anything about that night other than to say he was glad to see Scott had recovered so well.

Scott, determined to put that whole night behind him, did not mention it, either. Instead, he filled Larry in on every play of the game so accurately, Wil couldn't help but tease, "I didn't know we had a sportscaster in the making sitting at our table."

Scott ignored him and instead demanded, "Well, are you gonna tell your mom, or do I have to do it?"

Nora looked at her son expectantly. "Tell me what?"

Wil blushed slightly and grinned. "Well, Coach told Scott

and me after the game that he was considering moving us to varsity next year."

"Honey, that's great!" Nora hugged Wil, then reached for Scott. "I'm so proud of you two."

"Varsity as sophomores," Larry mused. "Pretty impressive stuff. Maybe you two could come out and teach my team a thing or two."

Besides ending his athletic year on a high note, Scott found a modicum of success with his academics. On the last day of classes, Ms. Frank settled her rowdy students down and stood before them, a paper in her hand.

"Class, please, may I have your attention? I would like to commend all of you on your effort this semester. Your final essays were quite enjoyable and well-written. I would like to share one of those essays with you. The writer said it was okay. It was certainly the best by this particular student, and it received the highest mark." She cleared her throat and glanced at the paper.

"'When we were asked to write about what we had learned during our freshman year, I am pretty sure my teacher wanted us to pick something from one of our classes or at least something that happened at school. But the biggest thing I learned this year happened outside of school. I learned about life, and how hard it is, and how rotten it can be, so much so that I wanted to run away from my life by just running away. But what I also learned about life is that there is a lot of good in it, and that a friend can make all the difference.

"'My home life wasn't the greatest. My dad is an alcoholic, and there were a lot of really hard nights to get through. Sometimes there was no food, and sometimes he could get really violent. I hated living with him because of what he was, but I always wondered if it wasn't some kind of sin to hate your dad. I tried not to, and I don't think I hate him even now, but it's very hard to love somebody like that. That was the rotten part of life, living with the yelling and the abuse and the drinking and the empty cabinets. That's what I wanted to run away from.

"'And then my dad burned the house down, and I ended up in the hospital, fighting for my rotten life. I didn't want to die. I knew that even before the fire trapped me in the attic. But I didn't want to keep living this same life. I wanted to live the life of my best friend. He's one of the good guys, the part of life that's good, the part that I wanted to get to and live in. He always offered to share his lunch with me when I didn't have any, and he always let me stay at his house on the nights when life was just too rotten at home. He always encouraged me to tell somebody. It's like he knew that the rottenness would go away if I would just ask for help. Sometimes I wish I had listened to him because it can be real scary waking up in the hospital when the last thing you remember is hiding in the attic from your dad. But then I think that I'm glad things happened the way they did, especially the part about me waking up alive and not waking up dead, because some of the good in life happened after the house burned down. My friend's mom gave me a home, a place where there's food on the table every night, and safe bedrooms to sleep in, and no yelling. And my best friend became my brother, and he still shares, and he still listens, and he still watches out for me.

"'I know now running away wouldn't have been the answer. I think I knew that when I was considering it. I also know that life is going to have its rotten moments; it's going to suck because that's part of the deal. But I also know that a friend like my friend can keep the suckiness to a minimum. I know that there really is good in life, and I know that, in the end, it's the good that will win out.'"

Ms. Frank looked up, and her eyes shined. She smiled as she handed the paper to Scott while the class, moved and amazed, stared at him.

"Well done, Scott. To give that anything less than an 'A' would be gross negligence on my behalf. I daresay you just earned a high enough average to manage a 'B' in this class."

Scott beamed at her while several students started calling out, "What did I get, Ms. Frank?"

"One at a time, one at a time," she said with a grin as she moved back to her desk.

Scott stared at his paper before tucking it inside his notebook. He looked up to meet Wil's gaze.

"It was good," Wil praised sincerely.

Scott shrugged, embarrassed. "I guess I was inspired."

Stacey Jo turned around in her desk, her eyes shiny with unshed tears. She leaned over and grabbed him in a hug.

"I think that was the just about the sweetest thing I've ever heard," she sniffled into his ear. Scott patted her on the back.

"So, do you want to go to the dance with me?"

"No," she sniffed and pulled away. "You're still a doofus."

Scott shrugged at Wil. "It was worth a shot."

But it was at the dance that night that Wil found the best things happening. He and Scott, dressed to the nines in their tuxedos, arrived around seven o'clock. Chris met them outside the gym.

"It's about time you got here," Chris chastised, straightening his tie. "My mom dropped me off a half-hour ago."

"Sorry," Wil apologized. "My mom insisted on taking about a hundred pictures. You'd think she'd never seen us dressed up before."

"What's the big hurry?" Scott asked.

"You are never going to believe who showed up with who," Chris teased, leading the way inside. The gym had been transformed into a blue and silver wonderland; balloons decorated every table and hung from the ceiling, streamers looped and twisted around the ceiling balloons and draped across the bleachers in a pretty pattern, and a blue "carpet" had been laid across the gym floor. Silver stars littered the floor and the table tops. An archway draped with blue and silver flowers stood in the doorway, and a large disco ball glittered from the center of the ceiling.

Music blasted from the speakers, and several kids danced underneath the disco ball. Many more sat around the tables, talking and laughing. Everyone had dressed as though this was the prom:

boys in tuxedos and girls in stylish dresses with corsages on their wrists.

Wil, Scott, and Chris spotted two familiar figures holding hands by the refreshment table.

"Whoa!" Scott exclaimed and laughed.

"Yeah, right? Derek is having a fit," Chris chuckled. "Come on."

The three of them made their way to the table. Andrew looked up at them as they approached, his fingers entwined with Laurie's. He wore a pair of khakis and a sports jacket.

"'Bout time you mutts got here," he said. "The chicken fingers weren't going to last much longer."

"Ooh, chicken fingers!" Scott exclaimed, grabbing a plate and helping himself.

"So, what's this all about?" Wil asked, pointing at Andrew's and Laurie's locked hands.

Laurie shrugged. "He asked, so I said yes."

"And Derek…?"

"Is Derek." She smiled. "He'll be okay. I know it's just because he loves me, and he worries."

Wil returned her smile and glanced at Andrew. "Well, I'll tell him not to worry. I think you picked a good one."

"Oh, I hope not," Laurie teased. "I like bad boys."

"Come on, you," Andrew growled, though his face flushed with pleasure. "Let's dance."

"Bye, Wil." Laurie and Andrew disappeared into the crowd on the dancing floor. Wil followed Scott and Chris to a table where Janet busily consoled Derek.

"Told you he was having a fit," Chris chuckled to Wil as they sat down.

"This is terrible," Derek fussed. "Uncle Frank is gonna have a stroke."

"Relax, dude," Scott said in between bites of the chicken fingers. "Andrew's not that bad."

"Yeah," Janet agreed. "Besides, Laurie really seems to like him."

"*That's* the problem." Derek shook his head.

"It's a *dance*," Janet reminded him. "What kind of trouble can they possibly get into?"

Derek sighed. "I guess you're right. You want to dance?"

"Sure."

"Good. This way I can keep an eye out."

"Charming," Janet muttered as he led her out into the crowd.

"Where'd Chris go?" Wil asked, looking around.

"He saw a couple of guys from the basketball team. Said he'd catch up with us later." Scott wiped his mouth and threw the napkin on top of his empty plate. "Now *those* were chicken strips."

Wil chuckled. "Can you believe it? We're gonna be sophomores."

"I never doubted it for a minute," Scott replied. "'Course next year, you might not want to cut it so close. Try to stay on top of your game from the get-go, like me."

"Jerk."

"Punk."

"Um, Scott?"

The two boys looked up. A pretty girl with brown ringlets stood in front of them. Her black dress flattered her tanned skin.

"Nina Selna. Hi," Scott stammered, a blush covering his cheeks. Wil bit back a grin.

"Hi," she smiled. "Do you … want to dance?"

"With you?"

Nina laughed self-consciously and nodded.

Scott jumped to his feet. "Yeah. That would be great."

She smiled and took his hand. Scott looked as if he had won the lottery, his eyes dancing and his cheeks bright red. Wil laughed and watched as Scott and Nina found a spot on the dance floor.

In fact, Wil watched a good many people do a good many

things—dance, eat, laugh, take pictures—while he sat there. The disco ball threw splashes of light around the room, and the music pulsed rhythmically from the speakers. Wil had just decided to get some punch just to have something to do when the spicy scent of cinnamon tickled his nose.

Smiling to himself, he looked up. Cassia stood beside his chair, radiant in a long ocean blue gown that matched the color of her eyes perfectly. A matching blue cord wrapped around her long hair, holding it place. She beamed at him through pale pink lips.

Wil stood. "I was hoping you'd show up," he said, studying her appreciatively. "Wow. You look...lovely." Scott had been right; it was the only word that did her justice.

"Thank you." She pointed at his tuxedo. "And this is a different look for you. I like it."

Wil shrugged. "It was required for the dance. You know, with it being formal and everything."

"Yes. The dance." Cassia turned her attention to the dancers. "A very interesting social ritual. This music is quite intriguing. Tell me, Wil, what is the purpose of this dance?"

"What do you mean?"

"Well, are we celebrating a birth? A death? A tribute to some god? Are we praying for rain or for divine intervention—"

"No, no," Wil said, waving her silent. "It's nothing like that. It's just a celebration. School's over, so everybody's just blowing off steam and having fun."

Cassia studied the room as the music switched to a slower, romantic tune. "Yes. They are definitely having fun. It is a very positive sensation."

She smiled at him, and Wil cleared his throat nervously.

"Do you want to dance?" he asked

"I do not know how."

"It's not hard."

"All right," she agreed and took Wil's hand. Harmony flowed into Wil as he led her onto the dance floor. That harmony broke for but a second while he pulled her hands up around his neck.

With some hesitation, he placed his hands on her waist and forced himself to exhale. He was quite certain she could sense his nervousness and willed himself to relax.

Cassia, for her part, seemed quite at ease. She spotted a familiar figure dancing close by.

"It appears as though Scott was not affected by me," she observed.

"Yeah. Whatever you did, I think it worked."

"Rayle's Feather of Forgetfulness is usually effective, unless that person is a true Secret Keeper, that is."

Wil couldn't help noticing that though her voice sounded light, she still seemed troubled when she looked at Scott.

"Is everything all right?"

"Yes." She looked at him and smiled. "I am ... just reflecting on my time here. It has been a worthwhile venture, do you not think?"

Wil grinned nervously. "You sound like you're leaving."

"I am. This is my final assignment, Wil. It is time for me to return to the clouds."

Wil stared at her, trying to rationalize with himself. He had known this day would come; he had just been successful at convincing himself he would be an old man when it did arrive.

Cassia sensed his disappointment. "I wanted to come say farewell to you and to Andrew. You have been a great help to my people, Wil. Your faith helped us re-establish our connections with this world, which means that Olin's blessings can once again flow down to your people."

"It feels like you just got here," Wil said. He saw Andrew and Laurie dancing nearby; Andrew watched him, a frown creasing his forehead.

"I know, but the truth is that many moons have risen during the course of my stay here. My people were never meant to live upon this earth, Wil. I must return to my home. It is time."

The song ended, and Cassia stepped away from him. "I must now say farewell to Andrew."

She left him and sailed over to Andrew, who excused himself from Laurie's side and followed Cassia into a quiet corner. Wil watched their conversation and saw the same expression of regret cross Andrew's face. However, Andrew seemed to agree with something she said, for he nodded his head and squeezed her hand after a moment. Then he stood and started away, pausing only a moment to look back at her.

Cassia's gentle look radiated loveliness as she smiled at him. Her gaze darted towards Wil, and she lifted her hand in a farewell gesture. Then she faded into wispy cloud and disappeared.

Andrew turned to make his way back to Laurie, pausing beside Wil. Both boys looked at each other. Andrew clapped Wil on the back and walked away. Wil stared at the vacant spot for a minute longer; he finally turned back to his table, hoping to lose his sorrow in the upbeat tempo of the music and gaiety of his friends, who seemed unaware of the dejection that had just settled over his heart.

WIL LAY ON HIS BED that night, his hands behind his head, his eyes gazing at the night sky visible through his open window. He was thankful that the dance had lasted until ten o'clock; that way, after forcing a cheeriness he didn't feel and telling his mom he had had a great time, he could feign fatigue and hide in his bedroom. However, his bedside clock read 11:37 p.m. and still he lay wide awake.

He couldn't believe she was gone. Life seemed empty now, emptier than it had before she had sailed into his life. The summer stretched before him, a hot, black hole devoid of any excitement. He couldn't think of anything but her absence: not the baseball camp he and Scott were going to in two weeks, not the job he would start in late July after the camp, not even what he would do tomorrow, the first day of summer break. None of those things held any interest now, not with Cassia gone.

He sighed and rolled over, staring at the dark poster that was Becky. Cinnamon apples swirled around his room. With a jerk, he sat up. Cassia stood in front of the window, her form glowing like soft moonlight.

"Greetings, Wil."

"I thought you were leaving," he said, his voice dumbfounded and relieved at the same time.

"I am. I have come to give you a draught." She held up a tiny vial of blue liquid.

"Why? What for?"

"So that you may get on with your life." She smiled reassurance at him. "It will erase knowledge of my existence from your mind—"

"No!"

"Temporarily," she continued patiently. "You are a true Secret Keeper, Wil. You have the ability to see us for what we truly are. No potion concocted by Samson can remove that ability. But to know of our existence would interfere with yours. You must be allowed to continue on your natural path. This potion will merely suppress the immediate consciousness. You will still know us when next you see us, and the knowledge you have gained will resurface at that time. I believe your people call it ... 'on-a-need-to-know basis'."

She held the vial out to him. Wil reluctantly took it from her fingers.

"But first, Wil, I have one more thing I would like to share with you." Cassia grinned at him and pointed to the ceiling. Then she vanished in a wisp of cloud and sailed out the window.

Gripping the vial in his teeth, Wil climbed out on the window ledge and hoisted himself onto the roof. He crawled up and sat down beside her. The moon hung full and huge in the sky, its light so bright that Wil could clearly see Cassia's profile as she gazed up at it.

"Wow," Wil said, turning his attention from her to the moon. "I've never seen it so large before."

In fact, he wondered that he hadn't seen it through his window. Cassia turned her blue eyes upon him.

"The moon can be a source of very great power," she said, her voice soft in the late night. "There is truth up there, wisdom and great peace."

"Yeah, I always thought the moon got the short end of the stick. I mean, everyone always pays such attention to the sun, I guess because of the light and the heat and the fact that it makes things grow. That, plus most people are awake during the day. But when the moon comes out, we're usually asleep, so we don't get to appreciate it that much. If people could see *this*, though, I bet they'd change their opinions real quick."

Cassia smiled gently at him. "I have no concern for you, Wil. You are going to fare well. You have defeated your banshee, and you helped Andrew defeat his."

"Andrew had a banshee, too?"

"Oh, yes. But your friendship gave him the strength to say no to her. Never doubt the power of friendship, Wil. It can mean the difference between lost innocence and virtuousness, between hurt and healing."

Wil thought about Scott's essay and smiled to himself. "Yeah, I know."

"Oh, look." She pointed at the moon. Wil followed her finger; a sliver of cloud drifted across the moon and seemed to linger, suspended in the air. Suddenly, he could make out the shadow of some creature running across the cloud, growing larger in the light of the moon. Wil squinted, trying to put together a name to the beast. Its galloping hooves came to a stand still in the very center of the moon, its profile large and clear. Its mane and tail blew in some invisible breeze, and off the center of its head protruded a long horn.

Wil gasped and stood up, his eyes wide at the image of the unicorn. Cassia stood beside him.

"You asked me once if the unicorn was real. The answer is yes. His existence is well-guarded by my people. You see, when the humans began turning their backs on the blessings of Olin all those moons ago, the unicorn was one of the first creatures to be affected by the cruelty of the men poisoned by Meslo's malice. They hunted the unicorn, caring not for his wisdom or purity but for the magic of his horn, magic which they did not know how to harness and which could never have been used for the greedy and selfish purposes they intended for it. This did not stop them from trapping and killing what ones they could and cutting the horns away."

Wil stared at her, horrified. The pain in her voice matched that in her eyes.

"Olin cried, for the unicorn was his most beloved of all creatures and one of his greatest creations. When Olin took away the ability to do magic from the humans, he also took away the unicorn. He realized man was not ready for the responsibility owed to such a creature, so the unicorn exists in the clouds until the day man is ready, and then Olin will return that beast to this world."

"Wow," Wil whispered, his eyes locked on the moon. The unicorn tossed its majestic head.

"He knows you, Wil," Cassia continued. "You could not have seen him except by his own choosing."

Wil gazed at the unicorn a moment longer, then looked at Cassia. "Thank you."

She smiled. "And now it is time."

Wil looked regretfully at the vial in his hand.

"Trust me, Wil. You will know me when next you see me. Until then, all this will seem as a dream to you. If you still doubt, consider the names Tolkien, Lewis, Beagle, and Rowling."

Wil gaped at her. "Are you telling me they're Secret Keepers? But they write about it! Is that allowed?"

"Of course, because they write about the *knowledge* of magic, not the art of *practicing* magic, which they do not know."

"Whoa." Wil stood amazed in this new information. Then he glanced at her and held out the vial. "How'd Andrew take it?"

"The same as you. With hesitation, but he did take it."

Wil nodded. "Do you mind if I hug you good-bye?"

Cassia's brow furrowed in puzzlement.

"It's what friends do when one of them is going away for a while," Wil explained.

"Of course," Cassia agreed, but she was surprised when Wil put his arms around her in an embrace. The serenity filled him, and the sorrow at her departure flowed into Cassia. After a moment, Wil let go of her and stepped back. Uncorking the vial, he closed his eyes and swallowed the blue liquid. It had a pleasant flavor going down and did not leave an aftertaste. He looked at her expectantly.

She smiled at him and touched her fingers to her forehead. "Farewell, Wil. Until we meet again." Her fingers arched down to her abdomen, and she faded into wispy cloud. As she floated for the heavens, the unicorn reared up in farewell and galloped into the shadow of the moon.

Wil sat back down and watched them disappear from his eyesight. The moon seemed to shrink to a more normal size; and the stars, which had been hiding in the brilliance of the moonlight, popped their heads out one at a time.

A light fog drifted over Wil's mind. He glanced around, surprised to find himself on the roof. His fingers rubbed at his forehead, probing some memory that had retreated far into the recesses of his mind. Try as he might, he could discover no reason that could explain his current location.

After a moment, he shook the cobwebs from his eyes and climbed back down the roof. Slipping back into his room, he stood in the middle of the floor, uncertain. He wasn't tired, though he knew he should be. In fact, he felt as if he had just awakened from a long sleep, a sleep in which the dream images were muddy and clouded.

He turned on his desk lamp, trying to distinguish between the real and the imaginary. His eyes fell on the unicorn poster, and he moved, mesmerized, to stand in front of it. Why did this seem so familiar? The unicorn, the girl, the moon? His foggy mind told him nothing.

His fingers reached out and touched the nose of the unicorn.

He let his hand brush against the hand of the girl seated before the beast. Unknown time passed as he stood there, finding in the poster a serenity that had never existed before. Stepping back, he saw something he had never seen before, something lurking behind the starfall touching the horn of the unicorn; he saw the magic.

It was there. It existed.

He sat at his desk and pulled out a notebook. Flipping open the cover, he smiled in understanding. He put the pen against the paper, and the language that poured out was half his, half the unnamed voice whispering from the clouded place in his mind.

"There is a place where the unicorn exists. No human can get there, for it is not on this earth. Rather, it is in the starlight, those twinkling spheres which glisten in night's blanket, that the unicorn lives and runs and plays freely. Its horn absorbs the light of the stars, or perhaps it is the horn that gives the light to the stars so that we on Earth may see them. And the unicorn is kept company by a girl whose face is moonshine and whose hair flows with the lightness of the clouds..."

LaVergne, TN USA
05 November 2009
163142LV00002B/19/P